BY PAULA SAUNDERS

Starting from Here

The Distance Home

Starting from Here

Starting from Here

A NOVEL

Paula Saunders

RANDOM HOUSE
NEW YORK

Random House
An imprint and division of Penguin Random House LLC
1745 Broadway, New York, NY 10019
randomhousebooks.com
penguinrandomhouse.com

Copyright © 2025 by Paula Saunders

This is a work of fiction. Names, characters, places and incidents are the product of the author's imagination or are used fictitiously. Any resemblance to actual persons, living or dead, events or locales is entirely coincidental.

Penguin Random House values and supports copyright. Copyright fuels creativity, encourages diverse voices, promotes free speech, and creates a vibrant culture. Thank you for buying an authorized edition of this book and for complying with copyright laws by not reproducing, scanning, or distributing any part of it in any form without permission. You are supporting writers and allowing Penguin Random House to continue to publish books for every reader. Please note that no part of this book may be used or reproduced in any manner for the purpose of training artificial intelligence technologies or systems.

RANDOM HOUSE and the HOUSE colophon are registered trademarks of Penguin Random House LLC.

Photos on pages v, 1, 45, 57, 83, 113, 147, 169, 245 copyright © 2025 by Kelly Winton

Library of Congress Cataloging-in-Publication Data
Names: Saunders, Paula.
Title: Starting from here: a novel / by Paula Saunders.
Description: First edition. | New York, NY: Random House, 2025.
Identifiers: LCCN 2025013587 (print) | LCCN 2025013588 (ebook) |
ISBN 9780593978290 (hardcover; acid-free paper) | ISBN 9780593978306 (ebook)
Subjects: LCGFT: Novels.
Classification: LCC PS3619.A8249 S73 2025 (print) | LCC PS3619.A8249 (ebook) |
DDC 813/.6—dc23/eng/20250411
LC record available at lccn.loc.gov/2025013587
LC ebook record available at lccn.loc.gov/2025013588

Printed in the United States of America on acid-free paper

randomhousebooks.com

1st Printing

First Edition

BOOK TEAM: Production editor: Evan Camfield • Managing editor: Rebecca Berlant • Production manager: Sandra Sjursen • Copy editor: Annette Szlachta-McGinn • Proofreaders: Emily Cutler, Caitlin van Dusen

Book design by Jo Anne Metsch

The authorized representative in the EU for product safety and compliance is Penguin Random House Ireland, Morrison Chambers, 32 Nassau Street, Dublin D02 YH68, Ireland. https://eu-contact.penguin.ie.

For my mother, who let me go—
and for my daughters, who reclaimed me.

Life was like that. Here you are, it said, and then immediately afterwards. Where are you?

JEAN RHYS, *Quartet*

PHOENIX, 1973

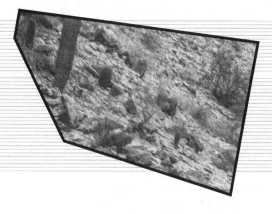

All the Right Reasons

1

Though Al objected to the idea of his son traipsing around in a tutu, Eve enrolled Leon in a local dancing class, figuring that since Leon was always tripping on the playground and running into things, ending up with stitches, concentrating on where his body was in relation to what was around him would be good for him.

Of course René wanted to do everything her older brother did. But she was too young for school, too young for dance class. So she'd skip and hop, twirling around the living room as Bobby and Sissy polka-ed through the champagne bubbles on *The Lawrence Welk Show,* Al's favorite—making Al chuckle and Eve stop whatever she was doing to laugh along.

"Always hogging the spotlight," Eve would say, shaking her head as Leon let the screen door slam behind him and took off on his bike to meet up with the neighbor kids.

Years later, after Leon and René had been studying together night after night at what may have been the world's most unlikely ballet school—the only one for more than three hundred miles on the great, unbroken plains of South Dakota—René was in pas de deux class, turning, whirling through multiple pirouettes en pointe under the power of her brother's hands.

Leon was tall and strong with dark wavy hair and deep brown eyes, and he knew just how to keep her on balance—an unspoken, unerring bond linking their weight and movement, one to the other. And as she spun through rotations she never could have managed on her own, the world was reduced to a single point of light. Everything quiet.

Then glissade and lift, and she was flying. From there, straight into piqué arabesque, then tour jeté, Leon effortlessly setting her up onto his shoulder. And after a mere blink of suspension, she was diving headlong, nose-to-the-ground, Leon catching her at just the right moment, placing her directly onto her pointe for a single beat of sublime, trembling balance.

Was there anything else like it on earth?

There was not.

Leon was teased at school, called "twinkletoes," "pansy," and worse—even by teachers—and willfully ignored by Al, whose attention he craved.

Al smoked and paced and worried whenever he was home, off the road for a few days between cattle sales. No one was ever particularly happy to see him. He and Eve fought day and night. Mostly about Leon: Leon's friends, Leon's hair, Leon's dancing. Especially Leon's dancing.

But when René danced, they'd stop their bickering to

cheer her on, whatever was wrong between them left behind for a moment of peace and camaraderie.

So she'd grand jeté and chaine through the house, trying to lighten the mood, while, in the fallout from one of Eve and Al's regular shouting matches—"You don't listen, Eve. I've told you a thousand times!" and "What do you want from me, Al? You're never around. *I* do everything. *Everything,* for God sakes," and "Oh yes, *everything*. Like turning your son into a ballerina. Just where do you imagine we live, Eve? What part of the country?"—Al watched *The Carol Burnett Show,* smoking cigarettes down to the nub, Eve slammed pots and pans in the kitchen, the youngest, Jayne, played quietly with her Kiddle Kologne dolls, and Leon, who'd given up dancing by the end of junior high, simply disappeared, skipping school to raid the liquor cabinet at one of his new friends' houses, to kick back with a bottle of whiskey or tequila.

Eve had met Al when she was just fifteen and he was twenty-two, home from air force training. She'd graduated valedictorian of her high school class, but instead of going to business college like she'd planned, like she'd always wanted—to become a personal secretary, a "professional girl"—she'd married Al on her eighteenth birthday. "How stupid was I?" she'd say again and again, charging through the house with a dust rag or the vacuum cleaner, shaking her head. "So stupid. Jesus Christ. A bona fide *idiot.*"

It was René's dancing that made Eve proud—that made them both proud. Eve bragged about it to her bridge club, and Al went on about it to the other cattle buyers at the livestock auctions in Philip and Fort Pierre. And René was talented. She knew the thrill of controlling her body, of attending to detail, of marshaling the power to cut through space.

So she'd been sent away to Phoenix. Not because the fights she and Eve were getting into were suddenly turning fierce and incomprehensible—Eve blaming her for how unfair it was that she "got everything" and Leon "got nothing."

No. She'd been sent away for one reason and one reason alone—to become a dancer, to "make something" of herself, as Eve said it.

And now, in Phoenix—living with an unfamiliar family, in an unfamiliar house, on an unfamiliar road—she was making a new beginning. Like in the fairy tale, she just needed to spin straw into gold.

2

A STREET RAN BY THE HOUSE WHERE SHE WAS staying in Phoenix, the house where she lived, the house where Eve and Al were paying "good money" for her to be. She didn't know what street it was or what part of town it was in or whether it followed a river or led to a highway.

The house was in the country, or nearly in the country. At least, there weren't any stores or other houses nearby. Not that she could see. It seemed like maybe there was a railroad. At night she imagined a freight train running right across the street, which she knew it didn't do. But it was definitely in the country because there were lemon trees in the back and grapefruits and limes, plus a stone walkway that led to a little cottage where a grandmother lived, though René had never seen her.

There have to be neighbors somewhere, she thought. *Maybe way down the road where the cars disappear?*

But she was too young to drive, and the parents at this house never continued down the road in front. They simply turned left out of the driveway, rounded the nearest corner, and went straight ahead onto a street that was empty but for large warehouses set off in dusty fields dotted with sparse bunches of what must have been cactus. And suddenly—instead of far-off jagged mountain peaks like back home—there were low-slung strip malls popping up, multiplying, coming to line both sides of whatever thoroughfare they'd ended up on.

3

ALL HER LIFE SHE'D BEEN TOLD SHE WAS BEAUtiful. In summer the sun streaked her hair with gold and sprinkled her nose with pale freckles, and her mother said she was beautiful and her grandmother said she was beautiful and everyone she met seemed to comment on some aspect of her appearance—her dark blond hair falling down the length of her back or woven into two long braids, her long legs and lean build, her dark brows and long lashes, her blue-gray eyes and Cupid's bow mouth and sweet smile.

"Well, isn't she a picture. Isn't she a beauty! Look out. Hahaha," people would say, winking at Al or giving Eve a look of warning.

And she was all right. She was good-looking, for sure.

But no matter that everyone seemed to agree that a girl should be at least pretty enough to attract a stranger's attention, she could see now that, for her, being "pretty" was going to be complicated. Because the dad at this house in Phoenix— who was thin and hairy and supposedly an orthodontist, though he never seemed to go to work—sat every night in his chair pretending to watch television as he snuck sidelong glances at her in her white cotton nightie. Every night, after she'd changed out of her ballet clothes, he trained his eyes on her as if she were the fox and he'd gone a-hunting—scratching his head and thighs with abandon, enormous flakes of dandruff raining onto his bathrobe as he ogled her through thick Coke-bottle glasses, grinning and blushing.

"He's taking time off," the mom told her quietly one morning, seeming to be both apologizing and attempting to explain.

Though René hadn't asked why the dad sat in his chair day and night like that, she'd been wondering.

"He had a heart attack last spring and he's very weak," the mom whispered, pouring milk into a serving pitcher.

And strange as he was, René felt sorry for him. Not just because of the heart attack. She could see how his whole life must have been. Lonely. So she figured that, under the circumstances, she shouldn't mind if he looked at her that way, piercing the thin white of her nightie with his big round eyeballs. But she did mind. It bothered her. She'd only brought the one nightie, since there were other, more important things she'd needed to pack when she left home. And it was white—not sheer but not *not* sheer, either.

Still, the mom's explanation clarified one thing, and René began to understand why they'd agreed to let her live with them here—wherever this actually was—in the first place. Despite the blooming succulent garden, the hearty fruit trees, the meandering pink stone walkway, the lush green vines winding up to the awnings, with the orthodontist spending whole days in his leather recliner in front of the television, they likely needed the money Eve and Al were sending.

The mom was a tall German-looking housewife who kept her hair in a long, smooth roll at the base of her neck, ear to ear, like a croissant, and maintained a constant cheerfulness, wearing a grin that wasn't really a grimace, though it often seemed to René that it might be. She kept to an internal code of conduct and had a simple way of being nice while at the same time making you notice that she wasn't losing her temper.

But the grandmother—who lived in the little cottage at the end of the pink stone path, just beyond the grove of citrus trees—was only for the real children, *their* children: a younger boy, Heinrich, called Henry, and a girl René's same age, Galiena, called Gali, who was in both René's ballet class and her class at school.

Catching sight of René in the school hallways, Gali would lean into her circle of friends and laugh into her hand, clearly whispering about René's tall knee-highs and too-long uniform skirt, since the rest of the girls at Mother Mary Ignatius wore shoes with no socks, in defiance of dress code, and skirts hemmed up to just under their bums. She'd perform the gesture even when the other girls didn't join in, even when it caused them to look at her skeptically.

And she applied variations of the same at ballet class, pulling girls close to make side-eye remarks about her new roommate—about the way René's leotard fit low and flat around the tops of her legs and high around her neckline, like some "dancer from the olden days," or how René pinned her two long braids across the top of her head for class, in what René's own grandma had called a "golden crown," but which too easily suggested the name Gali made sure René overheard: Rebecca of Sunnybrook Farm.

4

RENÉ HAD PROMISED NOT TO CALL HOME MORE than once a month, to help save money, so she ended up living with this new family—the Sheads—for a number of long weeks before finally picking up the phone and dialing the operator, placing a fictitious person-to-person collect call, asking for "Mary," as Eve had instructed, then—after hearing her own mother's voice say, "There's no Mary here"—hanging up and standing suspended in the kitchen, hand locked around the receiver, waiting for her mom to call her back.

She grabbed the phone from the hook mid-ring.

"So expensive," Eve groaned. "Good grief. We're going to have to keep it short. Well. How are you, honey?"

And after Eve had relayed the news from home—she'd been reorganizing the sewing cupboard, baking cookies, wallpapering the bathroom, while René's little sister, Jayne, who'd just turned ten, had been going door-to-door, collecting old coats for the Mother Butler Center—René talked quietly, cupping a hand over the receiver and whispering into the kitchen wall, glancing over her shoulder to make sure no one was coming in.

"The mom's nice, but the dad's creepy," she said. "And the girl here doesn't like me. She's mean to me."

"Give it time," Eve told her. "It's good of them to let you stay. You have to remember that. It can't be easy having a complete stranger in the house."

René didn't answer. She didn't know what to say.

Just a year ago, when René's old dance teacher from back home, Mrs. G, had retired and moved away, Eve—who'd become close friends with Mrs. G, working hand in hand with her to put on *The Nutcracker* every year, and who felt that by now she certainly knew the difference between a "good" and a "not good" ballet teacher—had quickly started bad-mouthing the new teacher, talking to anyone who'd listen about her "lack of training" and "tacky performances." Which meant that it hadn't been long before René was told—firmly, caustically—that she was "no longer welcome" at the only ballet school in the western half of the state.

So after a whole year of no dance lessons, she'd spent the summer down in Phoenix, living with Mrs. G and taking classes with Mr. Boyle, a serious ballet teacher Mrs. G had scouted for her. When summer was over and time came for her to go back home, back to school, back to *no dancing,* the decision was as simple as an on-off switch. It was "now or never," like Mrs. G said. If she wanted to dance, she had to stay in Phoenix.

"She has a beautiful talent," Mr. Boyle told Eve. "I'd hate to see it go to waste."

And since they couldn't very well expect Mrs. G to host

René for the entire school year, Mr. B offered to find housing for her with one of the students from his ballet studio.

Hence, the Sheads.

"I don't see any alternative. Do you?" Eve was saying now over the phone.

René shook her head, causing the long cord to twist and swing.

"Not unless you want to give up and come home."

"No," René said.

"Well, then—"

After another silence—which René could hear was causing Eve to think about all the money this phone call was costing—Eve added, "You need to give them a chance. I'm sure Gali doesn't mean any of those things."

And maybe Eve was right. Maybe Gali wasn't ignoring her out of spite, maybe she wasn't trying to get those other girls to laugh at her. Maybe she was just looking over, then quickly turning her back because she was worried René would try to insert herself at school like she'd done at home. Still, even after just these first few weeks at the Sheads', René understood that—far from being a welcome addition—she was an interloper, intrusive and galling. This was Gali's place, Gali's world.

And on Sundays, when only Gali and Henry got to go to their grandma's back cottage for brunch, it felt like a turn of the knife.

"Only *who?*" Eve asked, when René tried to tell her. "Go *where?*"

"To their grandma's," René whispered. "For breakfast. I'm not invited."

"Well, it's *their* grandma," Eve said. "And don't you want some time to yourself? Seems like you could find a good way to use it. Don't you have schoolwork?"

René sighed, lost. Of course she had schoolwork. The work they gave out at the Catholic girls' school she attended with Gali was beyond anything she'd ever gotten back home.

"Because it's a *prep* school," Gali had admonished one night when René fell into complaining on their ride home from ballet.

But *prep* meant what? René couldn't guess and didn't dare ask.

"Well, it was never going to be easy," Eve was saying. "You had to expect that. You had to know that when you left here."

"But—"

"Chin up, honey. We'll talk again in a few weeks. By then this'll all be far behind you."

René nodded, and they hung up.

But it wasn't going to be a few weeks. It was going to be another whole month before she could call home again.

"Oh, the usual," Gali sighed on her return from her grandma's that Sunday afternoon, holding her stomach and falling onto her bed. "Banana blintzes, chocolate crêpes, strawberries with whipped cream. Just stuff like that." And seeing René contract, Gali's eyes glistened. "Grandma said next time she'll make us a raspberry shortcake or a pecan roll with custard inside and caramel on top. Maybe I can bring you some."

Which, judging from the glimmer in her eye, she clearly did not intend to do.

5

THE NEXT SUNDAY, HEADING OUT TO HER GRANDma's brunch, Gali stopped abruptly and turned back, pointing a finger at her baby blue, pebbled-leather jewelry box with the large seashell perched on top, all pink and white. "I have to ask you to keep your hands off that while I'm gone," she started. "You didn't get into it last week, did you? Well, did you?"

Gali had short brown hair, cut like a boy's. She was large for a teenage girl, big-boned like her mom, with the sturdy, hardened physique of a full-time athlete—more like a discus thrower or a field hockey player than a ballet dancer.

"No," René said—startled, accused, her face coloring.

"I was missing the earrings I wanted to wear to school on Friday and I still don't know what happened to them." Gali crossed her arms and gave René a stern, probing look, like a prosecutor.

The Sunday past, René had held Gali's seashell to her ear to see if she could hear the ocean, like her own grandmother had always said, and she'd lifted the lid on Gali's jewelry box to peer inside, amazed at all the sparkling trinkets—gold and silver, beads and stones—each in its proper velvet compartment. But she hadn't taken anything.

"It's my good stuff." Gali raised her eyebrows. "I don't want just *anyone* getting into it."

So after Gali left, René decided to spend the morning outside.

She walked back and forth in the dappled sunlight between the garage and the far end of the driveway so that if one of them happened to glance out the cottage windows, they'd find her watching for cars on the unmarked two-lane, and she sat in the shade of the garage, examining the stones in the walkway, holding them up to the sky, looking for something she could see through, like a quartz or an agate, something familiar from home, suddenly feeling the weight of all she'd undertaken, of everything she'd promised to do and become.

If only she could have known how much she'd miss home—Eve and Al and Leon and Jayne. The longing was like an arrow running her through. Yet, she'd been chosen, set apart, sent away to accomplish something extraordinary, to bring back a prize—*herself*, but different, like a shining jewel. And she could do it. She could try her best, "give it her all," as Eve would say, until she achieved what she'd set out to do, until everyone was finally happy.

Hadn't others done difficult things? Hadn't René repeatedly heard the story of how Eve had been sent away from home at just thirteen, to care for the family of a woman who was sick and dying way out in the country—how she'd been bucked off her horse twice on the way, how she'd spent the summer wringing chickens' necks, killing rattlers, bringing broths and cool rags to the dying woman, all the while watching over the little kids and cooking dinner for the man? Eve knew what hardship was.

And Phoenix wasn't a hardship. Phoenix was an opportunity. So, no matter how she felt about it, going home was unthinkable. Not only would it end her hopes of dancing, it would constitute an unseemly failure, a failure for her whole family, a failure the likes of which even Leon's drunken escapades—plunging his car headlong over the guardrail into Rapid Creek, stealing Eve's fake pearl necklace to trade for a pack of cigarettes—had yet to achieve.

And wasn't she fifteen? Wasn't she grown up enough to look after herself, to shape the world the way she wanted it, like Eve said?

She had to remember that she'd crusaded to leave home.

Leon had been sent away a few years earlier, at about the same age as she was now, to a military boarding school in Colorado, in what Eve had called a "last-ditch effort to get him through high school."

It had been a dead end, since Leon had immediately gotten himself kicked out for stashing a bag of weed under his bunk—though he swore up and down it wasn't his. He'd ended up back at home, living like a mole in a damp corner of the unfinished basement for his senior year, mainly flunking out of school.

But unlike Leon, René had been sent off not because of all the trouble she was causing but—like the flip side of a coin—because of all she might achieve. Though she and Eve had been fighting over all kinds of things before she left, and though Eve was constantly complaining to neighbors and church friends, even store clerks, about what she brightly called the "teen-queen factor," Eve was proud of René.

To those René had left behind, the ones who'd had no choice but to remain—Eve opening her arthritic hands under hot water every morning, then working all day at her sewing machine or over the stove, Al driving countless hours to crack the ice on frozen cattle ponds or pierce his skin winding barbed-wire fencing—her departure must have seemed like a boon, a windfall, like something out of a picture book where a princess gets to escape from a locked turret and float, groundless, into some starry night.

"Sure," she wanted to tell them now. "You bet." Because what did they know about what it was like for her here.

And she raised her head, looking up at the windows of the little cottage, her mind drifting back to that breakfast party, imagining everyone happy and laughing, circled around a table piled high with sweets.

6

THE NEXT MORNING, JUST BEFORE DAYBREAK, René lay in bed listening to the call of the mourning doves. Hearing footsteps on the garden walkway outside the open window above her head, she rolled over, reaching up to see outside, thinking that if only she could meet that old grandma, the woman might like her, and if the grandma liked her, maybe she could go along to brunch, and if she went along to brunch, maybe Gali would reconsider and start to be glad she was around.

But no matter how she bent or arched, she could only catch the flash of the grandmother's silver hair or the hem of her nightie fluttering in the early light. No matter how she searched, the old woman stayed hidden among tree branches, reaching up to pluck a grapefruit, or all in shadow, bending to put it in her basket. And, giving up, René turned back, causing her bed to give a harsh, grating squeal.

It wasn't a bed, really, just an old World War II army cot wedged into a far corner of Gali's room.

When René had first arrived, the German mom and orthodontist dad had spent the entire afternoon digging through their garage to find it. They'd had to take it outside and brush the dust and rodent droppings from it before setting it up for her, in the corner, under Gali's window.

The first time René sat on it, the rusted coils sank straight to the floor, sending her feet flying as she grabbed helter-skelter for the side rails. She had to push herself up out of that hole and back to standing as the family watched—all of them laughing, hysterical. But she didn't mind. It was funny.

Then the orthodontist dad went running back to the garage to find an old door he remembered stashing there, while the German mom, still laughing, called out for him to stop, to "come back inside and sit down!" as she followed after at a trot.

When he finally returned, the orthodontist dad slid the old door across the metal frame, along the length of the cot. Then his wife placed a thin mat on top, and the whole family gathered around once more. And when René sat down—carefully this time—and didn't fall to the floor, they all whooped and cheered.

"What're you doing now?" Gali groaned, turning heavily in her soft, high bed. "For heaven sakes, can't you be quiet?"

Early on—way back, with the racket Eve and Al would make shouting at each other all night, screaming "Leon *this*!" and "Leon *that*!"—René had learned that it was sometimes best to move through the days without seeing what you were seeing, hearing what you were hearing, or feeling what you were feeling. And now what was most important was to somehow not end up getting sent back home before she even had a chance to get started.

So, though the hard wooden door beneath her felt like it was pressing right through her flesh, into her bones, she lay as still as stone and didn't answer.

7

THE MAIN PROBLEM WAS THAT IN BALLET CLASS René wasn't even in the running. She stood aside as other girls jockeyed for highest extension or greatest number of pirouettes, alert to the least shift in their pecking order—a girl who'd excelled at adagio was suddenly a good jumper, another who'd always been lyrical was gaining weight. She watched, searching for the slightest break, the slimmest leeway to ease herself into the game, all the while honing her skills: turnout, alignment, port de bras, extension. When the time came, she'd have to be ready. She'd have to work hard, to transcend her background. Despite the Phoenix girls' accumulated years of steady training, she'd have to find a way to surpass them—not only in execution but in precision and nuance.

And each day, as she stepped into the studio—taking her place at the barre, rolling up to her pointe, stretching her calves, not expecting to find friends, exactly, but hoping to see some match to herself, someone with whom she might sit shoulder to shoulder, hip to hip on a soft bed and compare extensions and arches—she could see that she was in the middle of a complication she never could have anticipated from back home.

The girls in her class may as well have been aliens. They were focused, trained, toned, ready to leap, twist, soar. Like her, they had in mind the perfection of form, of impulse and response. But looking at them was less like looking at flesh-and-blood humans than it was like looking at precisely tuned machines, less like looking in a mirror than like seeing something unfamiliar and threatening coming for you from far off down the road. And at the white-hot center of it all was their unyielding dedication to the hierarchy—girls moving ahead and dropping behind by turns, constantly challenging one another to either excel or fail.

Most remarkably, the girls were stick-thin and sculpted, with sharp angles, honed edges, unmistakable outlines. They were like line drawings—slight, single arcs of hip bones, cheekbones, ribs. And René understood that she was too soft and diffuse, her slender body too loose, her perimeter too amorphous and undefined. If she was ever going to join them—or even make them see that she was standing there—the first thing she needed to do was close the gap, starting with her own flesh.

She was going to have to remake herself to match them, become delineated from every angle like an anatomical model. Standing next to these other girls in her ballet class—with the marked exception of Gali, obviously the bull in the china shop—she saw that she was going to have to make herself indistinguishable from them, like a paper doll in a chain.

8

She started by refusing breakfast, stirring protein powder into water each morning as Gali gorged on French toast with butter and syrup, or scrambled eggs with bacon, or granola with berries and cream. She confined herself to celery sticks and a bite of tuna for lunch while the other girls at Mother Mary Ignatius wolfed down whole sandwiches, entire bags of chips, and bright packets of Twinkies. And no matter what the German mom made for dinner—Spanish rice with chorizo, sauerbraten and mashed potatoes, chicken and dumplings—she ate only steamed broccoli or green beans, no butter, no salt, recording each bite in a notebook, keeping track of the smallest indulgences—*Certs (10), gum (3)*—her mind the mind of an accountant.

When she got to five hundred calories for the day, she was finished. No matter what. Even when she could no longer face a flight of stairs, even when she knew better than to stand without steadying herself, even when violent cramps doubled her over right in the middle of school, her stomach seeming to digest itself.

One morning during algebra she raised her hand and asked to go to the school nurse, who told her to lie down, felt her belly, and gave her a Tums, which she quickly spit out and hid in her pocket: *Tums (10)? No.*

Her life here was finding a shape. She weighed herself in the mornings and again before bed. On a good day she could lose a whole pound.

So when her periods—which had started just the year before—stopped, it didn't matter. Because nothing changed the fact of those Phoenix girls and their long, ethereal silhouettes or what she needed to do to take her place among them. Nothing.

9

RENÉ AND GALI WERE UP EACH DAY BEFORE dawn—Gali screaming for René to "hurry up," hollering that she was "too slow," she was going to "make them late," they were going to "miss their ride!" But once they were out of the house, waiting at the corner for their car pool, Gali went silent. They stood apart, shivering and stamping in the morning cold.

Sometimes René opened a book, but she'd end up reading the same paragraph over and over, not registering a word—smarting from Gali's palpable dislike of her—before finally giving up and simply peering down the road at the oncoming cars.

"Looks like they're late," she tried one morning, hoping she and Gali might settle into something normal—nothing special, just regular.

"They're okay," Gali answered in an accusatory whine. "Don't worry so much. You're always worrying about everything. You think that helps? It only makes things worse."

Gali didn't actually look at René as she said this. Still, when she was done, she looked away, violently crushing a weed under her foot.

After the long drive to school—the radio blaring and the kids in front, whoever they were, shrieking about things she couldn't follow—René wandered class to class. And after school, as Gali disappeared to who-knows-where, she sat in the back corner of the library poring over the recipe sections of various women's magazines—lingering at photographs of roast pork loins and rib racks, plates of grilled asparagus drizzled with olive oil, sprinkled with sharp crystals of sea salt, perfectly burnt crème brûlées, magnificently caramelized tarte tatins, analyzing each one closely, then reading through the lists of ingredients as if, like a mystic existing on air, her grinding hunger might be sated by simply visualizing its fulfillment.

And when time came for ballet class, she walked the back alleys to the dance studio, talking softly to herself as she passed angry barking dogs behind chain-link fences, looking wistfully through the windows of the little houses to find kids watching after-school cartoons. Which brought to mind her little sister, Jayne.

Jayne—always making some fun. Like the time she did a headstand on a hillside snow bank and ended up plunging through the thin, icy crust, vanishing into a four-foot drift, only her snow boots and the ends of her plaid bell bottoms visible above the snow line. Luckily René and Leon had been there. They'd dug around the hole and pulled her out by her boots.

But Phoenix was different. Here, as René walked the shadowy alleyways, the whole world seemed to be happening outside her grasp, the simplest things—colors flitting across a distant TV screen, a kid's bike ditched in a patchy back yard—sparking quiet pangs of longing. On those long afternoons, when school was over and dance class hadn't yet started, she sometimes felt like a cartoon character who'd stepped off a cliff—wide-eyed, open-mouthed.

After the first few days of feeling hopeful and excited about being back in dance class again, about being part of a "new family," she knew better. In the same way that blackberries don't seed apple trees, cows don't birth chickens, ponderosas don't drop iris bulbs—in the way that things are made by God to generate more of themselves—as the weeks went by and she started to feel more and more disoriented and abandoned, she couldn't help but notice that it didn't seem to matter what she wanted or what anyone had planned. Things went their own way, picking up steam as they went along.

So, as if closing her fist around a magical amulet, she kept a picture in her mind of the day she'd finally return home to the folks she'd left behind. What she'd accomplished—her success, her delicate beauty, her renown—would lift them all up, carry them straight up to where they belonged without leaving anyone out. And that would be something to talk about and hold on to, something that would never fade or diminish. It would put things in order—everything finally justified, redeemed.

10

"STOP," MR. B CALLED ONE EVENING IN CLASS, clapping his hands together in the middle of a combination. "Stop." He turned to shut off the music. "Here," he said, coming over to René, taking her hand.

She'd been dancing every class from four in the afternoon to nine at night—double-checking her alignment in the slow pliés and tendus at the barre, forcing her extension inch by inch.

"Coupé, chassé, coupé, switch—" Mr. B explained, slowly marking out the steps, moving with her.

Gali—having arrived, as usual, from wherever she'd been, to join the last class of the day—turned and rolled her eyes, making the other girls in the advanced class grin and cover their mouths.

Mr. B froze. "Gali! Stop that," he said sternly. "You, too—all you girls. Pay attention. You all need this. Sharp! Not sloppy."

He let go of René's hand, restarted the music, and, checking to be sure she'd worked out the choreography and caught the timing, went back to pacing the studio, calling out the beat.

After class Mrs. Shead would be waiting outside in the car, ready to moan along as Gali droned on about her day—as if René, sitting silently in the back, hadn't put in ten times the effort. Gali always rode in front, leaving René mute and ghostlike, listening as Gali and her mom talked and laughed.

But even if they'd invited her into their conversations, René wouldn't have known where to begin. Besides, Gali and her mom talked mostly about college, which Eve had long ago ruled out, making it clear that René was "spending her college money" on dancing.

"Not everybody has to go to college, you know. Nothing wrong with that," Eve would say pointedly from time to time out of the blue—in the kitchen while she was scrambling to make dinner, in the TV room, hurriedly picking up and vacuuming, in one of the bedrooms, grumbling as she gathered dirty clothes to take down to the washer. Because neither she nor Al had gone, and they were all right.

At Eve's bridge club one night—as René looked in—Eve had suddenly groaned theatrically at the burden of having such a talented daughter and announced to her lady friends, "Since she's *insisting* on going away to study dancing, I guess it'll just have to be her *college education.*"

And all the ladies had laughed.

As if anyone else in this family is going to college, René had thought, standing there in the doorway, filling in what Eve had left out. Because Leon certainly wasn't going. After barely finishing high school, he'd hightailed it up into the hills with his drinking buddies to live in an abandoned cabin and chop down trees for the government. Or so he said.

So from the backseat of the Sheads' sedan, René listened as Gali and her mom debated the virtues of places she'd never heard of—Seven Sisters, Big East, Ivies—all the while reminding herself that the other girls in her ballet class, the real dancers, the ones not built like hockey players, talked mainly of quitting school and going for GEDs so they could spend more time in the studio, or not graduating at all, simply auditioning for ballet companies instead.

Back at the Sheads', the sky gone from morning dark to evening dark, she recorded her dinner—*half tomato (14), rice (40), peas (45)*—then lay on the floor in the narrow space between her cot and Gali's bed and did strengthening exercises.

Mrs. Shead had let her borrow a tape recorder, so even when she was blind with exhaustion, she only had to press play and follow her own voice: "*Développé up—and hold—and flex—and point—and lower, two, three, four—and hold, two, three, four—and lower—*"

If Gali happened into the room, she'd stop to make a point of peering down between the beds, amused and pitying. "Up-down, up-down," she'd say.

And René would smile, acknowledging the joke, her teeth clenched in the effort to lower her legs by intervals until her feet were hovering just an inch off the floor as she held on with her quivering core, battling gravity.

But maybe not all that funny, she'd think as Gali left.

Because René was not only getting thinner, she was gaining control. Which wasn't such good news for Gali, after all. It wouldn't be long before René was keeping up—and more than that. Her extensions were getting higher, her arches stronger, her ports de bras more expressive and integrated. Her body was responding—learning, calculating, shifting. She could look in the mirror and see it all happening, everything she'd dreamed of, the potential everyone had seen in her blossoming right in front of her eyes, as if her spirit and flesh were merging, being born as one into light.

If Gali's as smart as she thinks she is, she'd muse, taking her heel in her hand and stretching her leg up over her head, next to her ear, *she'll stop smirking and start watching her back.*

11

THEN ONE NIGHT AFTER CLASS, AS THEY WERE all walking out of the studio—everyone soaked in sweat, René hanging back to catch her breath after endless repetitions of an explosive big jump combination across the floor—Terri, a girl with long red hair and double-jointed extensions, came up to her and whispered that maybe she should go see Dr. Ramirez.

"We all go," Terri confided.

"I don't think Gali goes," René said.

"Well—Gali. You know," Terri said, meaning that Gali had those thick, powerful limbs and that stout core. Gali didn't need to go. She was as strong as an ox and looked it, approaching combinations with muscle and heft in place of the sleek, invisible-until-it-hits-you heat lightning of the other girls.

The doctor could give René shots to keep her energy up while she lost weight, Terri told her. "It really helps with jumps and turns, anything allegro," she whispered.

And with the way Terri touched her shoulder, whispering

words like *we* and *all,* René understood that she was being handed a key. It seemed that, with her sudden weight loss, she'd made herself an equal to those other girls. At least her efforts hadn't gone unnoticed. And as the chosen recipient of this new information, she was in the game, right where she needed to be.

But each time René brought it up, Mrs. Shead hemmed and hawed, giving polite excuses and exchanging silent glances with Gali and the hairy orthodontist dad. Until finally, René was able to call Eve and make her case.

"All right. Fine," Eve said over the phone, exasperated not just with René and the added expense of doctor visits, but with whatever was going on at home—all of which, though now outside René's hearing, was never far from her ability to imagine. "But only if you think it's absolutely necessary. This whole damn thing is getting ridiculous. I give and I give and I give and what do I get? Nothing."

Which seemed completely uncalled for.

From the sound of Eve's voice, René could tell that she and Al had been fighting—perhaps about Leon and some drunken appearance or one of his bill collectors pounding at their door. Though they could also have been fighting about René. Al had been against the idea of sending René to Phoenix from the beginning, so the added doctor bills would definitely be falling on Eve.

"Lord knows you're already costing everybody here an arm and a leg. So, why not?" Eve went on, sarcastic and angry.

Then she gave up, sighing. "We'll just have to come up with some way to pay for it, I guess. Who cares about money, right?" She laughed—falsely.

It was unfair. If they weren't going to support her so she had at least a slim chance of succeeding in Phoenix, then what was she doing here? And though hidden somewhere deep inside she felt a door quietly closing, René kept her mouth shut and ignored Eve's mocking tone.

And the next Saturday after morning class, Mrs. Shead picked up Gali and René at the dance studio—Gali ordering Henry into the backseat with René, as usual—and they all drove down into a neighborhood of small, identical, box-shaped houses with parts of broken swing sets and rusted lawnmower pieces scattered at the edges of bare dirt yards, and bits of torn, faded ribbon here and there, tangled and flapping in the branches of scrawny brown trees.

12

Dr. Ramirez's office was in a square green house, like a sun-faded Monopoly piece, separated from the identical houses on either side by thin strips of brown grass and a chain-link fence. Mrs. Shead gripped the steering wheel, bending her neck to look up and down the deserted street. "Maybe we should just keep going," she laughed.

But she pulled under the sloping carport, so they all got out and went inside.

The waiting room was cool even in the desert heat. And as Gali and Henry settled into chairs—picking up faded magazines, crinkling them open under circles of light from old desk lamps—Dr. Ramirez stepped out from an unlit hallway.

He was handsome and angular with dark hair that lay close to his head in waves, like Al's. Over his brown pants and tucked-in checked shirt, he had on a doctor's coat with his name embroidered in green thread. And without the least formality—as if he'd known René since the day she was born—he said, "Well, mija, why don't you and Mom come with me."

"She's not my mom," René said plainly.

Mrs. Shead drew a breath and Dr. Ramirez raised his eyebrows.

"No?" he said. "Well, that's okay. That's fine. She can still come along, can't she?" And he led them into a small room where there was a pale green exam table just next to a rusted metal cabinet lined with instruments that looked like things from out of the glove box of Al's Buick back home, for inoculating cattle.

He closed the thin accordion door that separated the exam room from the waiting room, and as Mrs. Shead looked on, he talked to René slowly, patiently, jotting down notes. He felt her throat, listened to her heart, looked in her ears, then asked what she'd had to eat that morning.

"Water and protein powder," she said. "Plus half an egg."

"And the day before?"

"All day?" she asked.

He nodded.

"Water, protein powder, half an egg, half an apple, a third of a can of tuna fish, two celery sticks, steamed carrots."

"And before that? A week ago?"

"Same thing. Pretty much. Maybe broccoli. Plus Certs."

She'd been coming in under five hundred calories a day for a while now.

Mrs. Shead grimaced and Dr. Ramirez rocked back, giving René a wide-open look like a question mark. So René tried to explain about dancing—about needing to be thin but also keep up her strength, about ways she'd found to get around mayonnaise, butter, grain—hearing herself speak more than she'd spoken since she first arrived in Phoenix.

Dr. Ramirez stood, his head tilted in confusion and concern, like the RCA Victor dog on Eve's record albums. He rested his hand on René's knee as though he were afraid she might float right up off the table and into the air.

"I can help you, mija. But only if you promise to start eating better," he said. "Your body needs good energy, from real food. So I can help, but only if you eat. If you don't eat—" He stopped. "You have to help, too, you know. Understand?"

René nodded and Dr. Ramirez gave her knee a pat.

"We'll need to test your blood to start with," he said finally. He turned to the cabinet, took a sharp from one of the drawers, then stuck her finger, smearing the blood onto a slide. "I'll be back." And he opened the accordion door, shredding it along the bottom where it was already in tatters from repeatedly grazing the deep shag carpet.

When he returned, Dr. Ramirez talked with Mrs. Shead about René's anemia. He wanted René to take iron pills. And he wanted to give her a vitamin shot.

"To help with your energy—put some pink in your cheeks." He touched René's jaw with his smooth knuckle.

"Like you give the other girls?" she asked as he turned to go out.

He smiled, nearly laughing. "For you, little ballerina? The same, exactly. It's what you want, right?"

"Yeah," she said, smiling back.

So he disappeared, ruffling the bottom of the door again as it opened and closed.

"I'm not so sure this is a good idea," Mrs. Shead whispered

tensely, her face gone rigid. "You certainly don't have to go through with it."

"I think I should," René said, nodding. "I think I will." She was going to seal the pact with those other girls. She was going to be one of them—like blood brothers.

"I don't think your parents are going to like it." Mrs. Shead was shaking her head.

"They'll be fine," René said, though she knew very well how Eve and Al felt about it. They didn't like paying for doctors, not even when Jayne woke up with pink eye or hives all over her body. Well, too bad. Because what did they know about what it was like to be down here with so much to do and no one to turn to? What did they know about what she might need?

Dr. Ramirez came back and gave René a shot. Then he took her hand, placing a small brown packet of iron pills in her palm.

"These'll do you some good, cariño," he said, closing her hand in his hands. "But you must eat. Real food. Promise me."

And with the way he said it, looking at her so kindly, she felt better already.

They stepped back into the waiting room, then followed Dr. Ramirez into his office—the only other room in the house, small and paneled like the exam room but with a desk and two folding chairs—where he continued to talk with Mrs. Shead about René.

"Let's see how it looks in a week," he said, wrapping up. "And you," he added, pointing at René. "You know what to do. Right, mija?"

So Mrs. Shead got out her billfold and started counting out money.

When they were back in the car the questions started: Did René's parents have any idea how much this was going to cost? Did they know she had to see the doctor every week? Her answers—*no* and *no*—ignited a flurry of glances between Gali and her mother, Gali even turning to the backseat to include Henry.

But René had just talked to Eve a week ago. It would be almost a month before she could call home again.

Back at the house, she overheard Mrs. Shead telling the orthodontist dad about the run-down neighborhood, the mystery inoculation, what a "quack" she thought the vitamin doctor likely was, and how, since René's family had no insurance—and even if they'd had insurance she couldn't assume the illegitimate-looking doctor's office would be qualified to take it—it was going to be costly. That was the main thing. It was going to be expensive.

Still, Mrs. Shead drove to Dr. Ramirez's every Saturday, leaving Gali and Henry in the darkened waiting room while she went in with René. It was always the same—talk, blood draw, vitamin shot, iron pills, counting out money.

René couldn't really tell if the shots and pills were helping. She was definitely thinner, noticeably more angular—her collarbones and hip bones jutting forward like the other girls', leaving Gali to eat her dust, she told herself—but looking in the mirror, twisting, she could still see folds at her waist, and when she bent, her belly still wrinkled. Could she be thinner? But she was so tired!

"Be patient, little ballerina," Dr. Ramirez said each time. "And eat! Remember? You made a promise. You trust me, mija?" Then he smiled at her—only her—and laughed, giving her a hand down from the exam table.

And, though she knew she wasn't about to give up her hard-won place by eating more than she was already eating, she was willing to be patient.

After all, it might be that Dr. Ramirez—who looked into her eyes and held her hands, calling her "mija," "cariño," "little ballerina," and who didn't have a single reason to dislike her—was giving her just what she needed.

13

WHEN HER KNEES STARTED GIVING WAY—twisting on the slightest impact, painful and uncertain—Mr. B said it was likely just growing pains. He taught her to wind Ace bandages in figure eights, under and over her kneecaps, and told her to eat: "French fries, hamburgers, milkshakes!" Then he pointed at Gali and shouted, "Not you!" Which caused Gali to gasp and turn so red that René almost felt sorry for her, and which guaranteed that René wasn't going to touch any of those things.

And as Thanksgiving closed in, Eve started saying, "You'll be home in just a few weeks for Christmas anyway. It's only a weekend, after all. No use wasting all that hard-earned money on airfare."

So René sat silently at the Sheads' dining table as the family laughed and ate, even the grandma—who, after all the anticipation and mystery, was nothing but a big disappointment. Like her son, the hairy orthodontist, she snuck sidelong glances at René through thick Coke-bottle glasses, shifting uneasily in her chair and clearing her throat.

Passing the green beans, she finally said, "So you want to be a dancer, too, do you? Well, you'd better get in line behind Gali. She's the dancer around here."

Which made Gali snicker and Mrs. Shead say, gasping, "Mother."

And René began to notice that the grandmother was gazing disgustedly at whatever bits of food René took onto her plate—*green beans (30), dry salad (25), tomato wedges (14), turkey slice (108)*—as though she wanted it all back, as though René were stealing the stuff right out of her mouth.

RAPID CITY, 1973

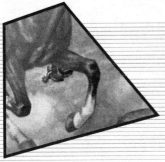

To Build a Bridge

14

After a seven-hour delay in Denver, René bounced her way back to Rapid City on a prop plane, the blades out her window working hard against a blizzard as the wing lights flashed, lighting up the storm. They skidded through snow drifts on the runway. Then men in insulated coveralls and trapper hats wheeled out a staircase, and she scrambled through the blowing snow in her suddenly ridiculous checkered shorts and light sweater.

Jayne spotted her first and started jumping up and down.

After giving her a hug, Eve took one look at her and said, "What in the world?"

"It was warm when I left," René tried, shivering.

"Well, I guess," Eve said, putting an arm around her. "My goodness."

"I got you a card," Jayne said shyly, hugging René around the waist and handing up an envelope. The card showed a cartoon man in huge construction boots, wearing an outsized newsboy cap, his hands clasped together at his chest.

"'How much did I miss you?'" René read aloud. She

opened the card and two enormously long arms popped out. "'*Thiiiiiiiis* much!'" she read, and everyone laughed.

Then Al shrugged off his heavy brown coat, wrapping it around her shoulders. "We were wondering what might of happened to you," he said, laughing.

Snow was blowing sideways outside the airport windows, whipping into whirlwinds, mini snow tornadoes popping up here and there across the open prairie. How quickly she'd forgotten about the South Dakota winters. Somehow, from where she'd just been, they were unimaginable.

Al picked up her bag and, ducking their heads against the storm, they went out, got in the car, and started for home, Al now in shirtsleeves.

"Brrr-rr," he said, giddy.

Home, René thought, taking a deep breath. She rode in the back, holding hands with Jayne as Eve turned and asked one question after the next—a happy barrage—and even Al chimed in, saying how brave René was, how proud they all were of everything she was accomplishing, while Jayne came up with plans for playing games and making snow angels and walking to Dairy Queen for Buster Bars.

"Yes, even in the cold!" she said against Eve and Al's protests. "It's not that bad. We can wear snow pants." And she smiled up at René so hopefully that it made everybody laugh.

Home.

15

WHEN AL OFFERED HER A PIECE OF HIS HOMEmade fudge, René declined. And when Eve made fried chicken with vegetables, mashed potatoes, and gravy, she took one carrot and two sticks of celery. She was determined not to go backward over Christmas, not to lose her hard-won edge by indulging in things like chicken and potatoes and fudge. As if those extra pounds weren't the first thing Gali was going to look for when she got back.

And it wasn't long before Eve started going on about how inconsiderate it was for René to be insisting that they spend money on a doctor when she was refusing to eat, how it was her own doing, after all, and she needed to take responsibility.

"I have the feeling you wouldn't even need that dumb doctor if you'd only be reasonable," she said from her sewing table one afternoon, pinning decorative flower patches over the worn spots on Jayne's jeans. "It's not fair, you know. It's not fair to any of the rest of us. No one else here is ever going to have the kind of opportunity you have. And it isn't cheap, you know. You've got to make the most of it!"

Eve paused, taking the jeans to her sewing machine, lining the patches up with her needle.

"Besides," she went on, "it's selfish to refuse the food put in front of you. Do you have any idea how many people would be grateful to have a meal every day?" Raising her eyebrows, she turned to René. "And just how do you plan to carry on, anyway, if you're not going to eat?"

René thought she could try to explain, but the words kept floating somewhere out of reach and nothing came.

"Well?" Eve said, looking at her, steely.

"Well—" René started. She stopped, unsure how to begin.

"I thought so," Eve said. "Well, you'd better start thinking about it. That's all I've got to say." And she turned back, pressing the pedal, running her sewing machine, then stopped, adjusted the feed, realigned the denim, and started again.

"I don't know what's the big deal," René finally said when Eve paused to round the next corner. "I have to diet. I just do."

"For one thing"—Eve turned to her, suddenly livid, like a match catching fire—"with your periods stopped, you might never be able to have children. How do you like that?"

She was looking at René in that way she'd so often looked at her before René had left home, her familiar hot glare sealing the notion that whatever was happening was somehow René's fault—Al storming around, Leon drunk, gone, yet still wreaking havoc.

Which put an end to any hope René had of trying to explain.

Still, when Al offered her a slice of Velveeta, a spoonful of molasses, a bite of caramel corn, she said no.

Unlike Eve, Al just nodded and turned away, shuffling and

humming to himself as he left the kitchen—as if he either couldn't imagine how it was his problem what René did or didn't eat, or as if he were sick at heart to have to add her to the growing list of things he didn't have one idea what to do about.

16

After the first few awkward dinners at home—saying no to the dishes that were passed, pushing around the small mound of salad or peas on her plate as the others looked on—René stopped coming down to the table. Instead, she'd stay in her room, pressing her face into her pillow to cut the wafting smell of meatloaf with ketchup glaze, or tuna-noodle casserole with crumbled potato chips, or green peppers stuffed with hamburger and toasted breadcrumbs.

Then one night—after Eve had hollered up the stairs, as usual, for René to come to supper and René had called back, "I'm not hungry!"—she heard Al rising from his chair, his cowboy boots ringing sharp and determined across the kitchen linoleum.

"René!" he bellowed up the stairwell. "You get down here!"

She didn't move.

"You get yourself down here. Right now!" he called again.

He stopped shouting when he saw her at the top of the stairs, but he was serious. "You come down and sit here with the rest of us," he told her. "Right now. Your mother's made a nice dinner, and you're going to sit here with us and eat it."

So René went downstairs and sat at her place. Al sat, too. The only one missing was Leon. Still, his shadow remained—like a dark spot they all agreed to look away from, a place that should have been filled with love and joy, now empty of everything but shame and sorrow.

"Now," Al said, putting on his formal dinner manners. "Who'd like some of this delicious roast beef?"

"I would." Jayne passed her plate and Al loaded her up.

"Eve?"

"Yes, please," Eve said, her face pale. She'd spent the whole afternoon making yet another big meal in honor of René's homecoming—chuck roast with carrots and potatoes, gravy, broccoli, salad, homemade dressing. Besides that, there'd been a phone call that morning asking for Leon, an old drinking buddy trying to look him up. As the guy on the phone tried to find out from Eve where Leon was "hid out," she tried to learn the same from him, thinking he might know. Half the time Leon was holed up in one of the local motels. It was only reasonable to assume that somebody knew where he was.

A lock of hair fell across her forehead, into her eyes. She swiped at it as Al dished up her plate.

"René?" Al said, raising the carving utensils.

Everyone looked at her.

"I'll just have a little vegetable," she tried.

Still gripping the oversized knife and fork, Al banged his fists onto the table, rattling the silverware, then dropped his head, exhaling like an untied balloon.

"I believe," he started, finally, as he rose up to gaze steadily, gravely, at René. "I *know*," he corrected himself, "that you need to understand something, René."

He was trying to stay calm, but she could hear what was buried in his voice. She remembered back when Leon was still living at home. With Leon either drunk or high, hanging out with the wrong crowd, flunking out of school, "wasting his life," Al's threats had been ongoing—the hammer permanently raised, permanently falling. And even back before all the trouble, back when Leon had been truly innocent of everything but a few nervous tics and a little attitude, there'd been that beating in the garage—Al taking a board to him, covering him in welts as he screamed. In the end there'd been no choice but for Leon to get out.

"*If*—" Al said to her now, letting the word reverberate. "*If* you don't start eating—right now, right this minute—you won't be going back to Phoenix. Do you understand me? If you don't start eating some of this good food your mother's worked hard all day to make for you—right now—you're going to be staying home with the rest of us. You won't be going anywhere. And that's final."

There was a long silence as Al took a deep breath and Eve sat stony, gazing at her hands.

"Now," Al went on, asking her again, formally. "René. Would you like me to carve you some of this good roast beef?"

René paused, blank.

Just like she couldn't recall the bite of a snowstorm from where she'd been in the desert, from here at home, there was no way for them to understand her situation down in Phoenix. There was no way for them to see how hard she had to work to fit in there, how every pound she kept off wedged the door a little more open for her, how food—exactly *not* eating it—was her lifeline.

So it seemed that only she could bridge the gulf that had sprung up between them. But to do that, she had to pay attention. She had to do what was required of her in these two disparate places. And she had to do it without making mistakes, without making any more trouble than she'd already made.

She lifted her plate. "Please," she said.

Eve looked up and almost smiled.

"Now that's what I call the right answer," Al laughed, slicing into the roast as Eve exhaled and Jayne giggled with relief.

After the meat, Al passed her the potatoes.

Then came gravy, broccoli, salad, dressing.

"Everything," Al told her. "That's the deal. That's the only deal. Everything."

And for René, it was like the breaking of a spell.

She ate. Happily.

For now, here with her family, she had no choice. For now, because of these people who—for good or ill—knew her, spoke to her, looked at her, and thought of her, who cared whether she lived or died, and who didn't have a single idea of the rigor required of her to even begin to occupy her "other life"—the one that made them so proud, the one they'd sent her away to inhabit and perfect—she was going to have to eat. For now, here at home, she was going to have to be her plain old regular South Dakota–girl self.

PHOENIX, 1974

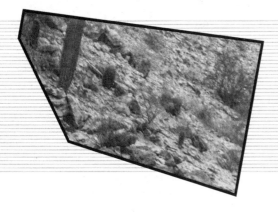

High Water

17

"I GOT FAT OVER CHRISTMAS," RENÉ SAID, SITTING UP in the front with Mr. Shead on the drive back from the airport. He was looking her up and down, so she figured that if only she was friendly he might keep his eyes on the road.

"I don't see how you could get *that* idea," he laughed, snorting, surveying her even more boldly, taking her in piece by piece as he drove. "You'd be a lot more to look at with some meat on your bones. That's for sure." Then he raised his bristly eyebrows, giving an involuntary whistle through his teeth.

She didn't answer. She already had the feeling of being ferried back into a burning fire. And talking to him only made it worse.

The days rolled by in an endless chain: Alarm!, car pool, school, library, alleyway, Mr. B, ballet class, ballet class, Gali, advanced class, backseat, stretch, pajamas, creepy dad, army cot, Alarm!

Little by little she was gaining ground. Mr. B didn't have

to stop the class to instruct her anymore, and she no longer kept to the back row for center-floor. Still, she was working the margins—driving her weight down while at the same time summoning the energy to dance, like wringing water from a stone.

She was nearly indistinguishable from the other girls now, her image in the mirror reflecting the same long lines, the same arcs, her movements matching theirs in clarity and beauty, her arches strong, lifted, her feet like gleaming points of light.

She saw Dr. Ramirez every other Saturday for shots and iron pills, though the visits didn't seem to help much. If she weren't existing on such a narrow ledge, she'd have given them up. But the last thing she needed was to lose her edge and end up back home, defeated.

And as the weeks ticked by, she became accustomed to being on her own. She wasn't looking for anything anymore. She'd given up on fitting in or belonging. Here, in Phoenix, it was going to be her, alone. That was a simple fact. So she accepted it, took it on. It simply *was*. And the loneliness and solitude began to feel more like penance and power.

One night, asleep on her army cot, she dreamed of Eve in a wedding gown, perched at the edge of a high bridge, leaning out over a rushing river. Seeing her mother tilted there above the swiftly churning water, she broke down, weeping inconsolably. She picked her way carefully across the narrow beam and curled into Eve's lap, her arms around Eve's neck, her tears flowing as Eve held her.

After a time, Eve spoke.

"You can turn your mind away," she said.

Just like that.

A revelation. A call to look beyond all the sadness and confusion, to train her eyes on the furthest horizon. She could shape her life not by what lay at her feet but by what she saw when she looked up to heaven.

That's what she was doing now, she told herself. She was turning her mind away. She was making her way.

18

THEN ONE DAY, OUT OF THE BLUE, SHE WAS INvited to Carly's.

Carly was small and sinewy like a gymnast, the slightness of her body making her head seem enormous. Walking into Carly's house, seeing the other girls from Mr. B's advanced class sitting around the huge dining table pretending to do homework as they talked and laughed, René instantly understood that, while she'd been alone in the library each day after school, the other girls, including Gali, had all been here.

There was a chandelier overhead—dangling crystals glinting sunlight into colored bands—and a lush green lawn in the back with a kidney-shaped pool. There was Carly's little brother, who kept rattlesnakes upstairs in a terrarium, as pets, he said—which Carly confirmed. There was a maid they called Birdie, who wore a clean gray uniform dress with white lapels, a starched apron tied snuggly at her waist, and who was working nonstop in the kitchen, just like Eve would be doing back home, preparing dinner: washing, chopping. Except that Birdie was making after-school soufflés. Carly seemed to be in charge of her and would take a poll around the table, then call out, "Cheese, Birdie!" or "Chocolate!"

"On the job, miss!" Birdie would call back heartily, as if her fondest wish was to make one soufflé after the other for Carly and her friends.

Birdie had her own small child with her there in the kitchen, a little boy, and René could hear her shushing and shooing him back into a far corner, telling him to stop pestering and stay out from under her feet.

Carly's mom showed up late in the afternoon—after "some kind of volunteer work," Carly explained, rolling her eyes, blushing and squirming. She gave a dreary hello, raising a hand to the table of girls as if to dismiss them, then headed into the kitchen to give Birdie instructions before retiring to her bedroom with a mixing bowl full of salad.

It was the home of people wealthy enough to be eccentric. And while the other girls lounged comfortably—draping their legs over the intricately carved arms of the dining chairs, even resting a foot on the tabletop—René was disoriented, as if she were playing a part in a movie she didn't have the script for. She didn't know what to say or how to act.

Still, she started coming to Carly's every day, sitting at the large table, copying the other girls' movements and speech patterns, reveling in the smell of Birdie's cooking, detailing every chasm and fold of soufflés as bright and high as top hats, then looking on as the others dug in and the delicate things collapsed, sinking into themselves.

And each day, as the girls went upstairs to Carly's room to get changed for class, René hung back. Carly's staircase was curving and endless. René couldn't imagine marshaling the energy to scale it. Plus, she needed a minute to collect the scattered pieces of herself, to put herself back together after trying in vain to follow the girls' insinuations and inside jokes, which she could never make heads or tails of.

Luckily there was a bedroom just off the kitchen, which Carly's family lent out to a cello student who was rarely there. So René would go in, shut the door, and soak in the quiet. She'd peer at the one small black-and-white photo on the cellist's low dresser, noting that, though his mother was normal height, he and his dad were freakishly tall, towering and thin, like men on stilts. And each day, she'd wonder how that lanky cellist felt here in this diminutive corner room, all by himself in a world full of people so comparatively short and solid. And she'd be sorry for him—for the way he was likely bossed around by Carly, just like Birdie, and for his having to be so far away from his family, wherever they were.

19

ONE AFTERNOON AT CARLY'S, RENÉ OVERHEARD Gali and another girl, Didi, talking about a dance competition that included prize money. Since prize money sounded like just the thing to make Eve and Al happy, that night she asked Mr. B about signing up.

And after spending the next few Sundays out in the driveway, reviewing an old jazz routine she'd learned from her dance teacher back home as Gali and Henry gorged themselves at their grandma's brunch, she won first place from the Phoenix Theatre Company Guild. They put her picture in *The Arizona Republic* and wrote about her being from South Dakota and about the five-hundred-dollar prize, which she sent to Eve with a clipping and a note saying how sorry she was for all the money she was costing them.

Didi came in second—which meant no money and no article. So, after that, Didi and Gali sat together at Carly's each day, whispering and shooting René mean looks.

Until one day, Carly—incapable of doing anything indirectly—looked up from her schoolwork and called out, in relation to nothing at all, "Hey, René!"

René looked up.

"Umm—" Carly hesitated, looking from one girl to the next. "I hear you took away Didi's scholarship. Umm—well—that's what I heard. And she won it last year, so really . . . it's kind of her thing."

Didi and Gali glared daggers at René as the rest of the girls sat motionless, watching.

"Well," René said, shrugging, "it isn't exactly *hers,* I guess. It's a competition, isn't it? That's what I heard."

"I guess so," Carly said, nodding. "I guess." And she left it at that.

But that night, on the drive home—René in the backseat, as usual, leaning her head against the car door with her eyes closed, picking up only fragments of what was being said up in the front—Mrs. Shead suddenly let out a sharp, hissing whisper:

"*Gali*! You stop that this *instant*!"

The radio was on and the two of them had been whisper-hollering. René had heard enough to know that Gali was complaining about her being at Carly's every day with the others.

"*My* friends," Gali whined acidly. "*My* ballet friends."

She seemed to be almost in tears.

René kept her eyes closed, pretending to sleep as Gali continued, incensed. "It's not fair. You don't understand. She's *everywhere* now. *Everywhere.* And *everyone hates* her. We *all* do."

The next morning, as they waited for their car pool, Gali made sure René understood that she'd only been invited to Carly's because Carly's mom had insisted.

"Nobody wants you there," Gali told her. "But there's no choice."

But later, from one of the other girls, René heard that it was only Gali who hadn't wanted her there, that Gali had vetoed every suggestion to invite René all year long, and that Carly's mom had finally said that it wasn't nice, that if they didn't invite René, none of the rest of them could come over, either.

So now René was at Carly's every afternoon. And though she still took to the cellist's small bedroom, happy to have a moment to herself as the other girls ascended the staircase—Gali glancing back to make sure she wasn't following—René bolstered herself by mulling over the facts. She was here. Just where she needed to be. Just where she'd wanted to be since she first arrived. She was one of them. Which was driving Gali crazy.

Good.

20

That spring, René, Gali, Carly, Didi, and the other girls from their advanced class were all selected as full performing members of the newly formed Arizona Ballet Theater. And after weeks of Miss M, the ballet mistress, shouting, "Legs up, girls! Steady! No bouncing!," they were in their white tutus and feathered headbands, in dress rehearsal at the downtown civic center.

Mr. B's daughter had flown in from New York to dance Odette, Queen of the Swans. His old friend—Edward Villella, a ballet superstar—had arrived to dance Siegfried. Mr. B himself was dancing Von Rothbart, the evil sorcerer, entering in a black feathered mask and shining black cape that he swung to cover his face, then tossed behind him, menacing and thrilling.

Now, as Miss M was giving final directions to the corps—René standing with the others onstage in full makeup, hands on her hips, bending this way and that to relieve her tired muscles and sore feet—suddenly one of the rear theater doors began to ease open. And though she'd known her mom was coming down for the performance, to René's astonishment there was *Eve!*, standing in the dark, silhouetted by light pouring in from the atrium. From across the vast ocean of seats in the darkened orchestra, René knew her instantly. It was no one else. It was Eve.

Eve tiptoed cautiously down the center aisle as if bewitched by the scene onstage—the flock of swans, the dark forest and painted moon, the lingering billows of fog from the dry-ice machine. She took a seat in the third row, grinning excitedly when she spotted René, clasping her hands at her chest.

And when Miss M finally dismissed the dancers—shouting after them, repeating for the umpteenth time that no one was to leave the theater until after the evening's performance—Eve stood tentatively, and René rushed for the footlights.

"Just where do you think you're going?" Miss M called out, moving to intercept her.

René stopped. "My mother," she said, pointing past Miss M, to Eve.

The only words she could muster: *My mother!*

So Miss M turned and, seeing the expression on Eve's face, seemed to register something so basic, so fundamental that it needed no explanation. She nodded and stepped aside saying, "No sitting in costume and no smudging your makeup."

René ran, squatting above the footlights, reaching to grasp Eve's extended hands. And though she felt she might burst, she didn't cry. With the thick layers of pale pancake on her face and the black liner above and below her eyes, she didn't dare.

Eve had on her light green pantsuit, her hair fixed up in a tall beehive—which she must have had done at the beauty salon in Rapid City, and which she would have had to wrap for the night before getting on the plane that morning. "Oh, honey," she kept saying. "Oh, honey—oh, honey—"

And they stayed like that, René nodding, grasping Eve's hands, saying, "You're here, you're here!," still trying to catch her breath from the shock of seeing her own mother right there in front of her, reaching up to hold on to her hands.

It was only a minute before Miss M was back, hovering. "All right. All right. Let's go."

"Good luck, honey," Eve said as René pulled away. "Break a leg!"

"Watch for me."

And René hurried offstage, disappearing into the wings as Eve waved behind her.

The other girls were already out of their costumes, standing around a table of food in their sweatpants or robes, helping themselves. And it wasn't just the girls gathered there. It seemed everyone who'd helped put the show together was digging in.

"Where's your mother?" Mrs. Shead said, coming up behind René.

"She left. She'll be back tonight."

"Oh—oh, my. Oh, dear," Mrs. Shead stammered. "Do you think she's already gone?" She pivoted and started trotting unsteadily down the hallway. First she turned toward the wings and disappeared. Then she crossed the hall to the stage door and pushed out into the sunlight.

When René was out of her costume and standing with the others, Mrs. Shead came up behind her again, sweaty and hyperventilating. "I couldn't find her," she said. "I'm so sorry. Oh, my. Do you have any idea where she could have gone?"

René shook her head, not understanding. For the first time since René had moved in with the Sheads, Mrs. Shead was unraveling.

"Lunch is for everyone. Your mother should be here. I meant to invite her. I didn't know she'd leave so quickly. Oh, my. I'm sorry. I'm so sorry."

And looking around, René felt a jolt of sickening clarity. It was true. The other moms—even some of the dads and siblings—were backstage for lunch, the other girls surrounded by their families.

To quell the sudden rush of emotions, she told herself that it was for the best, that Eve standing next to her here in Phoenix would be too much—there'd be too much to say, too much to think and feel. Yet Eve was so close! And she must still be nearby—just down the block in a rental car, or all alone in a café up the street. But René didn't know where she was or how to find her.

And recalling the longing that had filled Eve's face as Miss M had shuffled René backstage—seeing how it so perfectly matched the yearning René had been fighting all year—she knew it was her fault. Why hadn't she invited Eve backstage? Mrs. Shead had been backstage for every rehearsal. Why not Eve? Why did René still feel like an interloper, like she had to watch her step? What made her think she had to follow every rule, even when she didn't know what the rules were?

Now, even with Eve right here in town, it was the same as it had been all year long: Eve wasn't here. And René missed her all the more for the proximity, the lost chance.

She stood blank, stunned—as if hovering outside herself, floating untethered—finally forcing herself to mentally mark out her entrances, to go over the steps she'd rehearsed hundreds and thousands of times, to conjure the exacting postures and intricate details of choreography and timing until she was once again occupying her own space, standing where she was standing.

In just a few hours everything she'd been sent down here to do—everything she'd spent all these months starving herself for, working beyond her capacity to achieve—would be on the line. And it would require exactly everything she had.

So whether Eve was here or Eve wasn't here, René was here. And she needed to *be here,* ready—now more than ever.

21

WHEN THE PERFORMANCE WAS OVER—THE audience shouting "Bravo! Brava!" as the company took a number of extra bows—Mr. B called the corps de ballet into his dressing room, where he offered each dancer a yellow rose.

Handing a rose to René, he bowed slightly, taking her hand. "Well done," he said, as if all this time he'd sensed her struggle, seen her grit, as if she'd not only met but surpassed his hopes. "You were sensational, beautiful—a star!"

She beamed, her heart thrilling.

Yet with Gali in line right behind her, listening over her shoulder, she drew back. No doubt Gali would find a way to make her pay for this.

"I've imagined this night for a long time," Mr. B said to them all. "And I couldn't have dreamed of better. I guess we can go ahead and say it—" He paused, giving a big Hollywood grin. "We—were—fabulous!"

René turned to see Eve waiting shyly at the far end of the hallway, so she ran, still in her pointe shoes, and gave her a big hug.

"Oh, René," Eve said, holding a hand to her heart, her eyes misty, radiating waves of love and admiration. "Oh, my. I only wish your dad could have seen you."

Al and Jayne had stayed home because—"with all these damnable expenses," as Eve had said over the phone—there was no way they could afford to all come down.

"Wait here," René said. "Don't move." And, handing Eve her yellow rose, feeling her heart opening completely to her for-better-or-worse, one-and-only true mother, now standing timidly in this starkly lit backstage hallway, René ran back to the dressing room, got out of her costume, grabbed the suitcase she'd packed that morning, and still in her stage makeup, followed Eve out into the night.

Mr. B was closing the dance studio for a whole week, saying they all needed time to recover. And since it was spring break at Mother Mary Ignatius, Eve and René were going to Tucson to spend time with Al's mother, Emma, who was wintering in a little apartment over someone's garage. It was too late to show up at Grandma Emma's now, especially with the long drive. Plus, Eve wanted to meet Dr. Ramirez before they left town, to size him up and see for herself "just what in the sam hell" was going on.

So they spent that first night together at a motel Eve found on a nearby highway, and in the morning—still in the warm glow of the performance—they ate cinnamon rolls at a truck stop, then followed the directions Mrs. Shead had given them, driving across long stretches of open desert before finally turning onto the block of identical square houses and arriving at the office of Dr. Ramirez.

22

In the waiting room—the dim desk lights shining pale circles onto the wobbly end tables—René introduced Dr. Ramirez to Eve.

"*This* is my mother," she said, taking Eve's hand.

"Finalmente. The queen," Dr. Ramirez said, smiling.

Which caused Eve to stiffen and look him up and down, scowling—like, *What is it, exactly, you've been doing with my daughter? Taking her for a ride? Picking her pockets?*

Dr. Ramirez led them into the exam room, where he talked to René as usual, asking her about what she'd had to eat that week. But with Eve looking on, frowning, he was leaving out all the words she loved—*little ballerina, mija*—and keeping his hands in his doctor's coat, not anchoring her by her knee or shoulder like he normally did. He gave her the same shot, the same packet of iron pills, all the while acting like he'd never seen her before.

Back in the car, Eve put an end to it.

"All you have to do is eat," she said firmly. "That dumb doctor said so himself."

Eve was snapped back to reality. Any remnant of good feeling from the night before had evaporated.

"Whatever he's been giving you, it's over. I'm not falling for it for one more minute. Enough's enough. It's not like all these things are free, you know."

Though René resented the underhanded accusation—as if she'd been blithely passing out hundred-dollar bills to strangers on the street—she had to admit that she couldn't really say whether or not the shots were helping.

"Well, then," Eve said. "We can be glad to be out of that three-ring circus."

They spent the week in Grandma Emma's little upstairs apartment—René lounging on the couch, leafing through Emma's pile of *National Enquirer*s as Emma tempted her with everything from Oreos and Ho Hos to grapes and halves of avocados, saying over and over how René should just stay there with her, how she'd make lots of good things to eat and they'd go to the movies and have lots of fun, and how she wouldn't mind one bit missing all her senior center events, that there was nothing ever really going on there anyway, just a bunch of old people.

Then one day, after hooting about the "oldsters" at the senior center, Emma turned and looked pitifully at René, stroking her hair, and said right into her face, "She's having a hard time, isn't she. My girl."

Which made René's breath catch and her eyes sting. Because how could Grandma Emma see that when René's own mother couldn't? How could she possibly know? When she was little, René would cuddle in Emma's bed whenever they visited—the two of them whispering, singing, Emma telling stories late into the night as everyone else slept. Emma had taught her to count by fives, taken her out for raspberry sherbet, bought her copies of her favorite books. Somehow Emma could *see* it, and—with her grandmother bending to caress her—René felt weak, like she might just collapse.

Later that same day Eve made a show of putting her hands on René's shoulders, smiling proudly, looking straight into her eyes as if to infuse her with courage, and saying—loudly enough to be sure Emma overheard—"Just look at this girl, will you? Isn't she something? She's doing just great! She's so strong, and we're all oh so proud of her!" Then she folded René into her arms for a long embrace.

It wasn't just simple encouragement, like other moms might give. Eve and Emma had always been at odds, from way back before René was born. And though René now stood between them—embodying their divergent visions—there was no such thing as building a bridge.

The three of them went to the botanical gardens and toured the unpronounceable succulents and grasses. Emma walked with René to the library and let her check out as many books as she could carry. They went to the senior center for a potluck, where Emma introduced René to her friends, telling everyone how her little granddaughter from South Dakota was now living here, with a family in Phoenix.

And caught off guard by hearing herself saying such a thing, Emma turned quizzically to René, as if to say—*What are you doing down here, anyway? Why aren't you at home with your folks, for heaven sakes?*

When the week was over, Eve dropped René back at the Sheads' and left town.

René put her suitcase in the far corner of Gali's bedroom and lay down on her cot, bringing her knees up to her chest and turning to face the wall.

She was thin enough now, but she still had a long way to go. And she was tired, even after a whole week off. She was tired and lonely.

Sick and tired, she thought.

She'd heard the refrain all her life—as Eve washed windows or scrubbed floors or once again cleaned out everybody's junk from the back entry. But now she knew it in her bones. *Sick and tired.*

"Just keep going," she whispered, as if someone were listening, as if, after coming this far, there were any other choice.

She lay on her cot all day—careful not to cry. And not a soul came in to see about her, not even Mrs. Shead, not even at dinnertime.

23

RENÉ CAME INTO THE KITCHEN ONE DAY, AFTER the final pas de deux class of Mr. B's summer session—Mr. B running from girl to girl so that everyone got a turn with a partner—to find Mrs. Shead chopping onions. She thought maybe Gali's mom didn't hear her until, still facing the counter, Mrs. Shead said, "So are you planning to come back and study with Mr. B again next year?"

The knife hit the cutting board in a rhythmic staccato. There was no one else around.

"I guess so," René said, thinking, *What kind of a question is that?*

"We're going to be doing a lot of traveling next year," Mrs. Shead went on, sniffling. "So we won't be able to have you stay with us."

She set the knife down and turned to René, her eyes squinty, watering. "Onions," she said, laughing, running her hands under the faucet, then dabbing at her eyes with a Kleenex and blowing her nose.

"I'm sorry to tell you," she said. "We've been planning it for a long time, and it just won't work to have an extra person here when we might not be here ourselves." She smiled, but her eyes were glassy, hidden. "You understand."

What René understood was that Mrs. Shead was lying, that this was about Gali.

"That's okay," René said. And before she could think better of it, she added, "I'll find another place to stay. Maybe my grandma's."

It was a stupid idea—obviously unworkable. Grandma Emma was nearly two hours away, and she was only down in Arizona for a few months in the winter.

"That would be nice." Mrs. Shead smiled with something like pity. Then she turned back to the onions.

Not a week later René heard from Eve about a letter she'd received from the Sheads stating that the monthly payments Eve and Al had been sending hadn't even come close to covering the cost of housing René, and on top of that, they were still waiting on payments for some of the doctor's bills. They'd endured *too much for too long,* the letter said.

"Endured *what,* exactly, I'd like to know," Eve scoffed. "I've sent them every damn check for that dumb doctor. And they might've just raised the rent, for God sakes. 'No need to write back,'" she quoted from the letter. "'Just understand that we're no longer willing to continue.'" She stopped. "Do you think we need to send them more money?"

"I don't know," René whispered into the phone. "How would I know?"

"Exactly. How would I know, too?" Eve paused, sighing. "Well, it's too late now. And they haven't been the nicest family, sounds like, even right from the start."

And just a few days later, on René's final day in Phoenix, as she was packing her tights and leotards, leg warmers, ballet slippers, pointe shoes, along with her school uniform, trying to cram her whole life into one suitcase, Gali came into the bedroom and handed her a small thin square wrapped in blue tissue paper, tied with a yellow ribbon. A gift. Which was shocking.

René stood abruptly, taken aback.

"I don't have anything," she said, wondering if maybe all this time she'd misjudged Gali, if maybe René herself had been the problem, her insecurity and competitiveness getting in the way of what might have been a real friendship.

"Don't be silly," Gali said. "Just open it."

So René began to open the present, dazed by Gali's thoughtfulness, which was mysterious, heartening, even if their time together was at an end.

But with the first small tear of the wrapping paper, she knew. It was a wallet-size copy of Gali's school picture—a small blue square interrupted by Gali's tense, urgently smiling face.

"Oh," René said, confused.

"I wrote on the back," Gali said, bouncing gleefully on the edge of her big bed.

And instead of being filled, like before, with the wonder of possibilities, René felt herself contract, as if retreating from an oncoming blow. Because what in all this could be making Gali so happy?

She turned the photo over and read aloud: "'You're so quiet everyone thinks you're not smart.'" She didn't look up. "'But you seem to do OK in school tho. Have a good year even tho you can't live here anymore.'"

There it was. The Gali she knew. The Gali she'd lived with for almost a whole year.

She finally looked up. "Thanks," she said, empty of everything but convention. And she went back to kneeling on her suitcase, trying to get it zipped, ready to put this house, this family, this place—Gali's house, Gali's family, Gali's place—behind her. She was ready to go home.

RAPID CITY, 1974

Proving Ground

24

After René's first ballet teacher, Mrs. G, had retired and moved south to get out of the snow, Eve decided that, since the new teacher was "all but worthless," she'd start her own dance school in Rapid City, in a makeshift studio she constructed in their basement—plastering the ceiling, drilling holes for the barres, pressing stick-on mirrored tiles on the walls. Now, home for August break, René went down there to practice entrechats, cabrioles, grand jetés on the linoleum-covered concrete, checking her cracked reflection in the mirrors. Mostly, she ended up scraping her knuckles on the low ceiling and stopping mid-combination to keep from running into the walls.

Things were different at home since she'd left for Phoenix. To start with, Leon—a reliable font of trouble—was long gone, working on logging crews up in Spearfish and Deadwood, even as far away, they'd heard, as Wyoming and Montana. Which left Eve and Al, who no longer wrangled over Leon's endless pandemonium, happy to live their lives with as little intersection as possible, and Jayne, who'd learned from the experience of her older siblings that she was better off just doing what she was told, then hightailing it out of the house, to play at the neighbor's.

So it was peaceful, the way an ICU is peaceful—peace and quiet as both a respite and a matter of life and death. Besides the pop of a slice of bread coming out of the toaster, the whirr of Eve's sewing machine from the basement, there was hardly a sound, as if—along with Leon and René—all the turmoil that until now had constituted the main framework of their family had simply packed up and moved on.

And thank God, René thought. Because what she wanted most was for things to be peaceful. Just normal.

She ate popcorn and watched TV. She ate snickerdoodles, pancakes, turkey sandwiches, chipped beef in cream sauce over Texas toast with the rest of her family. She sampled Al's homemade fudge and downed a slice of Eve's angel food cake with defrosted strawberries. She rode bikes with Jayne to the local pool then to Dairy Queen, where they ordered Buster Bars and swung across Mount Rushmore Road to Wilson Park, to sit in the grass and watch the cars go by.

And in just two weeks she gained four pounds. *Four pounds!* When she looked in the mirror, the face that looked back seemed as round as the moon.

Since the Sheads had sent her packing, leaving her with no place to live in Phoenix, there was a lot of talk about what her options might be.

"Maybe just forget it," Eve said one day as they passed on the stairs. "Maybe just stay home with the rest of us. How about that?"

But if René stayed home, her ballet career would be over before it started. Besides, Eve would expect her to teach in that makeshift dance school down in the basement, plus in all the little cattle towns around Rapid, where Eve lugged her ballet records and record player each week to a rented hall, to coax the town kids through their steps. And nothing was as upsetting to René as the thought of spending her life propping up Eve's paltry dance school business.

Though Eve had starred in her senior musical at Fort Pierre High School, she'd never had any real dance training. So she'd depended on René to teach for her since René was twelve. Before leaving for Phoenix, René'd had to spend every Saturday driving with Eve to some distant outpost like Kadoka or Pringle, where she'd go over first position, second position, tendu, pas de bourrée—on repeat—with a bunch of farm kids who couldn't care less. Long before she left home, she was sick of it.

On the drive out, Eve would ask René questions about ballet steps that confused her—about the difference between a coupé and a cou-de-pied, a pas de basque and a pas de cheval, en dedan and en dehors.

René would answer, trying her best to clarify but all the while wondering, *How can you start a ballet school when you don't know anything about it?*

Then, after a full day of teaching, they'd have the long drive back to Rapid. Though they'd start by singing along to the radio, they'd always end by fighting. Before René had left for Phoenix, their fights had swelled into straight-out brawls.

"If you want to teach ballet so bad, why don't you just do it yourself?" René had ventured one day on their drive home from Murdo. She'd been maybe thirteen, and she was tired from the long day—from getting up early to drive two hours, from clearing the chairs in the hall and sweeping the floor and setting up the little portable barre, from having to wait through Eve's baby classes, where Eve put on music and told the little kids to "trot like ponies" and "jump like frogs," and from trying to get kids older than she was to at least point their toes. "Why do *I* have to do it? Why not just leave me out of it?"

"Jesus, you're such a complainer," Eve said. "Just like your dad. Always making a problem. You should be thankful, you know. For everything—everything you're just *handed,* I might add. For *free.* Good grief. If only *I* had it so good."

"*Free?* What's free? I have to work every weekend. Every Saturday. All day long. That's not free!"

"You're getting paid, aren't you? What could you possibly have to complain about, I'd like to know. What other kid do you know who has a good job like you do?"

"No kid. None! 'Cause it's *illegal*!"

"You're ungrateful, René. That's what's the matter with you. This'll be your business one day, you know. *I* certainly never had this kind of opportunity when I was your age. I never had anything just *handed* to me, that's for sure."

"I don't want to teach! I *never* want to teach! I told you that. But you don't listen. That's what's the matter with *you*! God!" René kicked the glove box, rattling the latch.

Eve drove on, pretending to be impervious. Then, after a few miles, she said, "My mother always told me I'd have a kid who was ten times brattier than I was. And look—! Here you are! A goddamn spoiled brat!"

After that, they'd been silent, René glaring at the open land speeding by outside her window as Eve drove.

So if René stayed home now, no doubt she and Eve would end up fighting the same battles they'd been fighting before she left, things exploding between them like dry kindling catching fire. And though she knew that once she went away again she'd long for home and everything about it, she couldn't begin to imagine what it might mean—for all of them—if she stayed.

25

"SHE'S GOT TO COME BACK. SHE HAS A REMARKable talent—magical, really. But she's just getting started. She needs to build her technique, to get stronger."

Mr. B was calling every day, talking to Eve until her ear was numb. He'd had no idea René was having trouble at the Sheads', he told her. "If only I'd known. I wish she'd have said something."

Which, when Eve relayed the message, made René groan audibly, because—*really*? How was she supposed to say something like that? It would have sounded like bellyaching, and everyone involved would have denied it. And what could Mr. B have done, anyway? The Sheads had made up their minds about her quickly and unanimously. They weren't going to reconsider.

So Eve was spending a lot of time on the phone in the basement—where she was also doing laundry and catching up on the alterations she'd started taking in from a menswear store downtown. Every time René went looking for her, Eve was down there, the telephone cradled awkwardly between her neck and shoulder as she reached to pin a seam or fold a pair of trousers.

"Good God. I think my ear's going to fall off," she'd say when she finally hung up, bending her neck and rubbing her shoulder.

Then one night, when all the lights were out and Jayne, René, Eve, and Al were all in their beds, the phone rang. After about the third ring, Eve jumped up and ran down the stairs in her nightie.

"What? Slow down. Where are you?" René heard her say. "*Where?*"

René went to sit on the steps, to listen.

"Come get me," she heard Leon shouting over the phone line. "Com'on, Mom."

"You've been drinking," Eve said matter-of-factly, holding the phone away from her ear.

"I think so. Yeah," Leon laughed.

"So where are you, Leon?"

"Rockerville. You know Rockerville, right?"

"Of course I know Rockerville. *Where* in Rockerville?"

"That old-timey saloon. They keep tellin' me I hafta leave but I can't go nowhere. Everybody already took off and just left me here. Shit."

"Well, stay there. Stay right there, Leon."

"Okay, Mom. I'll tell 'em you told me to."

"Just wait there. I'll be there as soon as I can."

Rockerville was half an hour away, up in the hills on the way to Mount Rushmore.

"I've got to go get Leon," Eve said, passing René on the stairs, frantic, rushing to change out of her nightie as Al snored.

"I'll go with you," René said.

"Hurry up, then. I'm not going to wait."

So René pulled on her sweats and they took off into the night, headed for the Rockerville Saloon.

Leon was just where he said he'd be, sitting all alone at a big round table meant for a dozen people. He was leaning back in his chair, looking up at the ceiling, crooning along to a song on the jukebox, keeping tempo with his fingers on the tabletop. When René tapped him on the shoulder, he jolted upright, ready for a fight. Seeing her, he groaned and melted back into his chair.

"Jesus, René. Where'd *you* come from?" He reached his arms out. "If I could stand up, I'd hug ya." He giggled as though he'd told a good joke. "Come 'ere, come on. Si' down. Where's Mom?"

"Right here," Eve said. She was standing just next to René. "All right. Come on, Leon. Let's go."

"Not yet," Leon said. "Jus' sit. Sit with me. Com'on. One more song."

Leon was well over six feet. They weren't going to be wrestling him out of that bar. Given the state he was in, it was up for grabs whether the two of them would be able to support him as far as the car.

Eve sat down. So René sat beside her.

"Here. Le's get a beer. Jus' one. Com'on. Jus' one. On me."

Leon flailed his arm in the air, as if he were calling a waitress, but the place was empty aside from the bartender, who was standing behind the bar, looking the other way.

"Where'd everybody go?" Leon laughed. "They were all here a minute ago."

"Come on, Leon. Time to go," Eve tried.

"After this song, jus' this song." Freddy Fender was playing on the jukebox.

"Okay. But no more."

And when "Before the Next Teardrop Falls" was over—Leon swaying to the music, nearly tipping out of his chair—they stood, one on either side of him.

"Okay, okay. I got it," he said, shooing them.

He pushed himself up and they each took an arm, guiding him out into the starry night as he hummed, staggering down the steps and through the dark parking lot. When they got him to the car, he fell longwise into the backseat. So they hefted his legs in after him, bending his knees in to shut the door.

"Thanks for gettin' me," he said, fixing his hands under his head for a pillow, closing his eyes. "I didn't know you were home, René. It's good to see ya."

And with that, he fell into a sleep likely just this side of kingdom come.

For the next three days, Leon was curled up on the couch in the living room, his back to the world.

Eve made him soups and grilled cheese sandwiches as Al grumbled and stormed around the house, sometimes just shaking his head at Eve, looking like he was about to spit, sometimes jostling the couch in frustration, maybe to remind Leon that there was still a board somewhere out in the garage with his name on it, that even though Leon was now bigger than Al, Al could still give him a whupping.

"Get up, Leon," he said one afternoon, giving the sofa a hard kick. "You can't sleep it off forever, you know. Get up and be a human being for once."

But when Leon simply turned his head and moaned, without even opening his eyes, Al stomped out of the house and left town, likely headed for a Motel 6 in Winner or Presho or some other town filled with cattle pens and grain silos.

Finally, after three days of sleeping as if in a coma, Leon stood up from the couch, his face puffy, his eyes dark and glassy, like he'd been in a car wreck. And just a day after that, there was a friend of his out in the driveway, honking his horn.

Leon hugged Eve and Jayne, saying goodbye as though he'd just stopped in for tea. Then he turned to René. "Don't be a stranger, okay?" he said.

"Okay." She smiled, wondering what he was talking about. "You, too," she said, reaching up for a hug, holding on, remembering how he used to balance her in promenade and catch her when she came flying into his arms.

Then he started for the back door, headed back up to Rockerville, he said, to pick up his truck and hit the road.

"Looks like I mighta missed a few days of work." He shrugged. "I better get going."

"Stay away from that stuff, Leon," Eve said to him. "You know how to say no. Just believe in yourself. You can do it."

Leon laughed. "Okay, Mom. Don't worry." And he took off, smiling and waving, letting the screen door slam behind him.

Eve waved after him, watching Leon from behind the screen, going pale as the pickup pulled away. Then she sighed and slumped down onto a step in the back entry.

"I think I'm going to be sick," she said.

Still, after a few minutes, she stood and started slowly back down to the basement, to catch up on her sewing, while Jayne took off for the neighbor's, and René went out to sit by the big tree in the front yard, wondering what might happen next.

26

"She could try Larry Dicker in Denver," Mrs. G said to Eve over the phone, long-distance. "He's first-rate, a good friend from way back at Sadler's Wells. I could call him, Eve, see about setting up a meeting, maybe get her an audition."

"She'd be closer to home, at least," Eve said. "That'd be a plus. And she could drive herself to Denver, so it wouldn't cost so damn much. Or she could just stay home. That'd suit me fine. It'd be nice not to have to drain my bank account every month."

"We'll figure it out, Eve. I'll look into it and get back to you. Just don't give up. Hang in there."

"All right," Eve said. "Que será será." She laughed but she wasn't a bit happy about any of it. René was in the kitchen sitting across from her and could hear the worry in her voice.

"Denver's as good an idea as any," Eve said after she hung up. "Who knows?" she added. "What we really need is a crystal ball. There's just no way to know."

But there was one way. Because Mr. B kept calling, frantic, saying that *he* knew, he knew beyond the shadow of a doubt.

"If she goes to Denver, she'll never dance," he told Eve, straight out. "She won't get the training. And this year is important. Critical. I know that teacher in Denver. And I don't like to talk badly, but I've heard things. He's got a certain reputation. Let's just say that. If she goes to Denver, she'll be lost. She'll lose everything. You can't let her. You can't let her do it. She's *got* to come back. I'll find a place for her to live. I will. She *must* come back."

But no one who'd grown up like Eve—saving herself from generations of poverty and ignorance, from a life knee-deep in river muck and farm work by following her own whistle, listening to her own tune—liked it when somebody tried to tell them what to do. In fact, they disliked it so much that, most of the time, they did the opposite.

As Mr. B and Eve talked on and on, René sat on the front steps, timing Jayne's footraces with the neighbor kids, eating chocolate chip cookies and lime Popsicles, rhubarb muffins and lemon bars, each day lending a new roundness to her hips, a softening of the lines of her thighs. For three straight weeks she'd given in to every temptation: *Food, so much food!* Now—with three, four, five extra pounds!—her hard-won spot in the Phoenix girls' pecking order would be lost. They'd laugh at her. She could already see Gali covering her mouth, gasping, as the other girls stared, wide-eyed. She knew the game. Five pounds changed the world.

Eve tapped her on the shoulder, holding out the phone.

"Mr. B wants to talk to you."

René stood and took the receiver inside.

"René?" And there it was—the warm voice of her teacher, who believed in her, who saw her for who she aspired to be. "We miss you down here. You know that, dear? Why didn't you tell me you were having trouble at the Sheads'? I would've wanted to know. You could've told me."

The line buzzed quietly.

"I don't know," René said, still unable to fathom how she might have brought up something like that. *They don't seem to like me?* That wouldn't even have made sense. She wasn't down in Phoenix for the Sheads to like her. It didn't matter what the Sheads thought of her. Until they told her she couldn't come back, of course. Then it mattered. "It was okay. It wasn't so bad."

"Now, you need to come back here," Mr. B said. "You know that, right?"

"Okay," she said, thinking, *No.*

She couldn't go back. She wouldn't survive the other girls' silence, their false pity, not to mention having to starve herself all over again, having to start from the beginning.

"This is a turning point for you, René. You need to come back here and complete your training. After that, I can line up something for you in New York. There are people I can send you to when you're ready, not before. But first you *must* come back."

"Mom's thinking about Denver," she admitted. "There's supposed to be a good teacher there, and I'd be closer. I'm old enough to get my driver's license now, and I can have my grandma's old car. So I could come home whenever I wanted. I'd get to see my family."

"You could fly from here just as easily, don't you think?" Mr. B countered. "I think so. Even easier."

"Okay," she said, thinking that he didn't understand about the money.

"You could go home more often if you needed to. We could arrange that. I know that teacher in Denver. I've been in this ballet world a long time, René. And people talk. I don't want to say too much, but that teacher has a bad reputation. You need to know that. He's known to use his students very poorly. They say he only teaches to meet men. Do you understand me?"

To meet men? That couldn't be true. Mrs. G knew him. She knew him better than anyone else did.

"Now, I don't like saying things like that—" Mr. B was suddenly gruff and serious, like when he had to make a correction he shouldn't have to make. "But I do care about *you,* and you need to come back here. If you want to dance, you need to come back, René, and keep going with school and keep going with your dancing. We'll figure out everything else. We'll find you a good place to live. Okay?"

"Okay," she repeated.

"All right?"

"All right," she said.

"Okay, then. I'm glad. We're all set. We'll figure it out, and we'll see you in a few weeks. Now pass me back to your mom, dear. We'll see you soon."

René passed the phone back to Eve and left the room.

"First of all, Denver's going to be a lot less expensive," Eve started later that same afternoon. "Especially since you can just drive back and forth. We can't forget about that. That makes a difference."

"But Mr. B says that teacher—"

"Mrs. G would never suggest someone who wasn't the 'best of the best,' I don't think. Do you?"

"No," René said quietly, wondering.

"And since Denver's so much closer, you can come home for Thanksgiving, for Easter, even for a weekend if you want to, if you feel like you need a break. That'd be nice, don't you think?" Eve was cheerful, smiling hopefully.

She'd been home for three weeks and no one—not Carly or any of the other girls, not Gali or Mrs. Shead—had called her. Not even to say hello. Plus, hearing Mr. B say that he'd find her a "good place to live"—like she was someone no one wanted! The only thing that remained of her year in Phoenix was her Mother Mary Ignatius yearbook with her class picture, in which she didn't look one bit like herself—her face drawn and gray, her hair thin and lifeless. But there was her name, and just above it, that photo—unrecognizable.

So, even if Mr. B managed to find a place for her to stay in Phoenix—some other family arm-wrestled into taking her in—Eve had clearly had enough of the expense, and René had plenty of her own reasons for never going back.

"I think Denver's going to be just the ticket," Eve was saying, buoyant. "We'll have to make a visit and see for ourselves."

27

They drove through Buffalo Gap, Hot Springs, Edgemont, then took a left at Mule Creek Junction—a barren T-intersection in an endless stretch of empty highway, land spreading out to beyond what a person could comprehend, everywhere deserted. Eve wore her sunglasses to cut the glare of golden grasses against a stark blue sky, and when it was time for lunch they didn't stop. They were meeting Larry Dicker at an amusement park he liked on the outskirts of Denver, and Eve wanted to get there before the sun went down.

They parked in a weedy lot behind the arcade, then trudged toward the blinking lights and tinny music. They were waiting on a bench inside the main gate, watching the crowd, when Eve spotted a diminutive man in a snappy pin-striped suit, his patent leather shoes reflecting the flashing neon. She jumped up, extending her hand.

Dicker stepped back, shifting his glossy walking stick and reluctantly lifting his hand, tilting his head in an aggrieved way as she introduced herself.

"I believe you've received my letters," Eve said brightly, smiling.

"Indeed, madam. I have," Dicker replied, already pulling away.

Eve tried to make small talk over the carnival noise as she and René followed Dicker to a metal picnic table in the food court, where girls in tank tops and boys in muscle shirts were devouring dripping nachos and foot-long hot dogs. And when Eve began to talk about René coming to Denver, Dicker nodded.

"I've seen the photos you sent," he said. "She's obviously talented. She'd be a welcome addition." He grinned coolly.

"But with all the extra expenses," Eve started, "like housing and school. We were hoping . . ." Her voice trailed off. "Perhaps—"

"I don't give scholarships." Dicker waggled his head at her. "Not to anyone. I believe I made that clear in my correspondence."

"Of course, yes—of course," Eve stammered.

Dicker was silent, unmoved, keeping his eyes on Eve.

"Well," Eve continued. "She'll be a long way from home, is all."

"It puts me in a bind, you know," Dicker said testily, raising his chin at her. "What would I say to my other students? Many of them have financial difficulties, too. And what if I had to offer all of them scholarships? Then where would I be? I'm sorry, but I have to be fair."

Eve nodded as Dicker—his translucent skin taut and shining, his mouth like the slit in one of those coin-operated carnival games they'd passed on the midway—abruptly dipped into the pocket of his fitted vest and pulled out a slip of paper.

"The address where René will be staying. If she so chooses."

He handed the paper to Eve, then turned and raised an eyebrow at René.

"Mrs. Babbitt's a very dedicated woman. Never misses a class. And I believe her daughter's around René's age. That should work for you all. You can visit in the morning. They'll be expecting you."

And with that, Larry Dicker nodded at Eve, tilted his head in René's direction, stood up, and left.

Eve and René watched, dumbstruck, as Dicker disappeared into the night.

"So, no scholarship," René noted.

Mr. B had given her a full ride in Phoenix—free classes, as many as she could handle, to help offset the cost of out-of-state housing and schooling. It was the least he could do, he'd said.

"Well. It's still going to be cheaper," Eve said, almost to herself. "School here's a lot less expensive than in Phoenix." She was musing, figuring. "That's one thing. Plus we won't have plane fares to worry about."

They began to stroll aimlessly around the carnival grounds, gazing blindly at the rides, both of them out of sorts, jangled and confused. The Ferris wheel was stopped, its rainbow neon blinking as the people stuck on top rocked forward to look down impatiently, like *What the hell's going on down there?* The roller coaster roared over their heads, riders screaming, as the Bullet soared and dropped, spinning.

"Mrs. G says he's the best," Eve tried. "I imagine she knows."

They stopped at the Tilt-A-Whirl, which was going full speed.

"You want to ride?" Eve said absently. "We're here. You might as well ride."

René liked carnival rides. Whenever the carnival came to Rapid, she knew very well what she wanted and what she didn't want. She liked riding the Tilt-A-Whirl, but if she had to sit by the door on the Bullet, she wasn't getting on.

Yet somehow at this amusement park in Denver—colored lights blinking in the dark, metal rides clanging, shrill screams rising over blaring carnival music—she couldn't come up with the least inkling of what it was she might want. Between going back to face those girls in Phoenix, and Mr. B and what he'd said about Dicker, and having to stay home and teach for Eve or leave and live with strangers all over again, she was scrambled to blankness.

"I think I've had enough of all this," Eve said, sounding disgusted. "You?"

René nodded.

"I don't know what in the world could have made him want to meet up in a place like this," Eve went on. "I'm more than ready to get out of here."

"Me, too," René agreed, wondering if Eve was also thinking about the men, about what Mr. B had told them regarding Larry Dicker's reputation.

And at just that moment, Eve said sharply, "Is that *him*?"

She pointed to the outline of a man in the distance, someone pacing the edge of a sparsely lit parking garage on the far side of the park. "That couldn't be him, could it? What'd he do? Leave one way and come back another?"

They squinted into the darkness but the man was too far away.

"Maybe I'm seeing things," Eve said, giving up. "I'm that tired. Just about dizzy."

So they walked out through the back turnstile, across the open field behind the arcade, and got in the car.

"Maybe this new family will be nice. That'd be a good change, right?" Eve said, trying to pep things up.

They drove to the nearest motel—broken neon announcing a vacancy—and got settled in a room. They'd visit the new family in the morning before getting back on the road and retracing the miles to home.

"Don't worry, honey," Eve said drowsily from across the narrow divide between their sagging beds. She reached up to turn out the light. "I'm sure it'll all look different when the sun comes up."

28

The "new family" was an older mother, like a grandma, and a daughter, who was a few years younger than René—maybe fourteen to René's just-turned sixteen. They were "music people," the mom said. "Opera." They'd all been "music people" until her husband had left, she told them, taking his part in it somewhere else.

"Not to the great *beyond*," the mom clarified, which meant, by the raising of her eyebrows, that he'd taken it to some other woman. "Oh, but he was marvelous!" she exclaimed. "My favorite accompanist. Life took him in a different direction, yes, but I can't complain. We always had such glorious music in the house."

And seeming to careen hopelessly, as if falling in love all over again, she leaned onto the dust-covered baby grand that took up most of their small living space.

The mom was a scarecrow—all elbows and knees—her straw-like yellow hair wrapped in a moth-eaten scarf, which accentuated the sharp contrasts in her pale cheeks and caused her large eyeglasses to protrude. She led Eve and René to the sunken-in davenport under the front window—Eve initially hesitating, brushing off the cushions in an effort to dislodge the layers of embedded cat hair—then served tea in mismatched, chattering teacups. And before long she was putting on a record and standing behind a rusted music stand, where she commenced singing Puccini—putting on an alarming vibrato and reaching for high notes with a volume that made the unseen birds in their towel-covered cages scream and the cats hiding under the furniture run for the back of the house—as the daughter, who'd all the while been silently haunting the narrow archway to the kitchen, simply grinned and shivered.

Eve was wide-eyed throughout the recital, and at the end she clapped and called out, "Bravo!"

René looked at her. No doubt Eve was a good sport.

But when they were finally back in the car that morning, Eve turned to René and, jamming the key into the ignition, whispered, "Good god. I mean. *Really*. And *that's* what that smell was about. I was wondering."

The scarecrow mom had shown them through the small, run-down house to a back bedroom just across the hall from where—she'd confessed shyly, abashedly—she shared a room with her dying father.

"He needs someone there every minute," she'd said, not opening the door. "He has a bell he can ring for me. Half the time it's in the middle of the night. Wouldn't you know." She'd laughed in what she must have felt was a melodious way—at herself, at human nature, at life, at death—and at just that moment, they'd heard the old man groan and cough, though he didn't call out. "He has a lot of pain. I need to be close by," the mom repeated.

The bedroom across the hall from the old man had a canopy bed with filthy, dangling pom-poms, the whole thing coated in decades of accumulated grime. You couldn't have touched that top canopy cover without sending up a cloud of choking dust.

"And this is Kat's room," the scarecrow mom said, adjusting first her headscarf then her glasses. "But she's giving it up so that René will have a nice place to sleep." She beamed, triumphant in their generosity.

René looked at Kat in disbelief, thinking not so much of how Kat was giving up her bedroom but of the horror of being expected to occupy it. She couldn't imagine sleeping in that foul, airless place for even a single night, let alone a whole year.

"You don't have to do that," she quickly said.

The girl stepped back, as if attempting to disappear into the wall next to her dresser, and grinned shyly, stymied by having been spoken to.

"I want to," she finally squeaked out.

"But where will Kat sleep?" Eve asked.

"We'll set her up in the basement," the mom said. "She'll be fine. Won't you, Kittykat?"

The girl nodded, and the mother and daughter—who shared the same bony frame, the same beaked nose, and were wearing the exact same eyeglasses, René noted—lifted their shoulders in exactly the same way and giggled.

"Well," Eve said. "It isn't necessary, but it's awfully kind of you. Isn't it." She turned to René.

"It is," René said as she blanched, unable to grasp this new fate. "But I can sleep in the basement," she tried. Because anywhere would have been preferable to this lightless hovel, the dank air so completely suffused with floating particles it seemed someone must have recently stamped out a campfire.

"*No, no, no, no, no, no, no,*" the scarecrow mom sang out. "It's all set."

"Do you think you're going to be able to stand it with all those cats?" Eve asked now, on the drive home. Eve hated cats. As a girl, growing up just next to the Missouri, her little burnt-grass yard had been overrun with cats. She'd taken a gunnysack full of kittens down to the river one day, meaning to drown them, but she'd flinched at the last minute. Watching the little kittens flail and cry out in the deep water, her heart had clenched and she'd jumped in after them. Still, her opinion on the subject was unchanged.

René looked out her window, watching the land go by, and didn't answer.

"I'm guessing you'll have a better time of it at the Babbitts' than you did at the Sheads'," Eve went on. "That's my feeling. They seem nice enough, don't you think? And the way that woman looks after her old father— Well, she's obviously a caring person."

Eve's verdict was that the Babbitts were odd but kind, "nonjudgmental." Which made sense, considering how strange they were.

René gave a long, deep sigh and kept track of the lengths of empty grassland, now turning to rolling hills.

If she tried to tell Eve about wanting to stay home but not wanting to teach in Eve's dance school, about wanting to dance but not wanting to leave home, not wanting to have to sleep in that filthy bedroom, not wanting to face all she was going to have to face at the Babbitts' or back in Phoenix—wanting, not wanting, wanting, not wanting—Eve would start in about her being spoiled. She could already hear it: *Even when you get everything you want, you're never happy. Just like your dad. Always something to complain about.* They'd be off to the races.

"How would I know if they're nice or not?" she finally said.

"Well, that's right," Eve said, reaching to find a station on the radio, circling the dial in vain. "How can anyone know? But as long as you work hard and stay focused. That's the main point, isn't it?"

Back at home Eve got a phone call from Dicker. He was willing to offer René a half scholarship but they'd have to agree to keep it quiet. If any of his other students found out, he said, he'd be forced to discontinue. Otherwise, half was fine by him.

Eve hung up the phone, raking her fingers through her hair. "Well, it's good to have that settled. And really, it's a nice gesture on his part."

René stood motionless. There were only five days left until school would start again, and there had been no word from Mr. B. Whether that meant that he hadn't been able to find a place for her to live, or that he'd been told by Eve that a decision had already been made, or that he'd simply given up on them, she didn't know. But Eve seemed happy that everything was set, that everything was finally decided.

"Maybe it'll turn out to be okay in Denver," René said, trying it on for size just a few nights before she had to leave. She was in the kitchen with Eve, chopping celery for the dinner salad.

Eve turned from the stove, where she was searing a chuck roast. She raised her voice to be heard over the sizzling meat, holding her metal spatula in the air like a scepter. "It'll be whatever you decide to make it," she said. "I know that much."

René nodded and turned away.

At least she could finally leave behind the specter of being humiliated by Gali and those other girls in Phoenix. Those Phoenix girls could go ahead and disappear just like smoke. There were other things she needed to think about now—like that scarecrow mom and her spooky daughter, along with the groans and smells of the man dying in the next room, plus Mr. Dicker, whoever he might turn out to be.

And later that night, gathering last-minute clothes from her drawers and stuffing them into her already over-packed suitcase, she decided that what Eve had said in the kitchen was surely true. She'd have to buck up. She'd have to make the most of it.

At least for now, she thought—trying to rein in her careening mind as she leaned over her bag, forcing an extra pair of socks down into a corner—*all I really have to do is pack.*

DENVER, 1974

Closer/Farther

29

Eve didn't have the energy to make the trip to Denver all over again, and Al wasn't around, having left just after they'd gotten back, saying he had important cattle business up in Montana. So René figured she'd take her grandma's car to Denver like they'd talked about.

"It's a heck of a long way, don't forget. You don't want to drive that all on your own, do you?" Eve said.

"No," René said. She didn't.

So Eve started asking around and found that the grandson of a bridge club friend was driving to Denver, that René was welcome to ride along.

"Hallelujah!" she said over the phone. "I can drop her off at your place and the kids can take off from there."

"And maybe you can offer half on the gas?" the friend said. "I know he could use the money." Which struck Eve as thoughtless, even rude, given that nine times out of ten she drove out of her way to give her friend, Mrs. Beech—who was older and had night-vision trouble—a ride to their bridge club games.

"I'll send along ten dollars," Eve said, barely able to conceal her irritation. "That ought to cover it."

On the morning of René's departure—well before daybreak—Eve came in to Mrs. Beech's house and, after a quick cup of coffee, hugged René and left her there with her suitcase. So René sat in one of Mrs. Beech's overstuffed armchairs in her pink-and-white-striped T-shirt and clean white jeans, her hair woven into two long braids, pretending to look through the *House & Garden* magazines Mrs. Beech kept handing her—the sky out the windows still black as pitch—as they waited on the grandson.

It was more than an hour before the grandson finally stepped out from the back bedroom, obviously having just woken up even though Mrs. Beech had been shuffling back and forth down the hallway the whole time, knocking on his door, calling out. He'd splashed water on his face and run a wet comb through his hair, leaving ridges. His black T-shirt was twisted, hugging his chest, showing off his large biceps. But in spite of his scruffiness—*or maybe because of it,* René thought—he was handsome, tall and swaggering, and René felt a sudden surge of excitement, as if the two of them were heading off on a wild adventure.

"I told you. I warned you!" Mrs. Beech started when she saw him coming down the hall. "You had no business running around till all get-out—"

"Calm down, Granny," her grandson said, tugging to straighten his shirt and throwing on a frayed denim vest. "No need to have a heart attack." He edged past her, jerked open the front door, then motioned to René. "Let's go, Candy Striper."

Which must have had something to do with her outfit.

"You get back here, mister," Mrs. Beech yelled at him, starting for the kitchen. "I don't care how late you are, you're not leaving without breakfast."

"Nope. No breakfast."

"Well, isn't that the *limit*!" Mrs. Beech turned and stamped her foot at him. "And you've made this nice girl wait so long—"

"Bye, Gran!" the grandson shouted over her, stepping back inside to give her a peck on the forehead. Then he took off out the front door.

"You behave yourself!" Mrs. Beech called after him. "You be a gentleman!"

"Got it!" he called back, raising an arm but not turning around.

So, after a quick goodbye, René followed him out, wrestling her suitcase into the backseat. She turned to wave as they started down the road—the grandson honking loud and long—and could see Mrs. Beech shaking her fist from the front porch. The sun was just beginning to shed a pale orange light across the far edge of the horizon, and all the neighbors' houses were still dark.

30

Mrs. Beech's grandson, Pete, said he was a radio DJ in Denver. And when René told him that he didn't sound like any of the DJs she'd ever heard, he put on his "professional voice"—dropping an octave and drawing out the vowels, fake-announcing the songs on the radio.

"Like two different people," she said, and he laughed, smiling at her like he thought she was clever, but also like he was already well aware.

They weren't even to Hermosa yet when Pete started calling out to her in his DJ voice, spidering his fingers across the bench seat between them to tickle her hand or tug on her long braid. He wanted her to scoot over and sit next to him, in the middle. He kept at it all the way through Buffalo Gap—crawling his fingers up to her elbow, her shoulder, her earlobe—until she finally figured she might as well make a deal with him.

"Only if you promise to keep your hands to yourself. You have to promise. No going back."

Pete took both hands off the wheel. "From my mouth to God's ear," he said. "Promise."

So she scooted over, close but not touching.

"Come on," he said. "Don't be stingy." So she budged over a millimeter more. Pete was older—maybe in his twenties—with rugged features, dark wavy hair, plus that deep voice hidden away inside, so she didn't mind.

By the time they got to Hot Springs, Pete was reaching over her leg to adjust the radio then dropping his arm, letting the weight of his forearm settle on her knee until she brushed it away—at which point he'd laugh, then wait a beat, then do it again. By Mule Creek Junction, as deserted as ever, he was stroking her thigh—up and down, up and down—stopping to grip her just above her knee, pressing his fingers hard into her flesh until she cried, "Stop, stop it. Stop!," which made him throw his head back and howl.

She knew well enough that whatever happened out here—where they may as well have been the last two people on earth—would be him against her. They both knew that. So she laughed along and made sure to cry, "Stop!" in a cheerful way to show that she understood that he was just goofing around, having fun. Because mainly she had to get all the way to Denver, and Pete had to take her there.

So, like that—with Pete doing his radio voice, grabbing for her, while she joked along, fending him off—the miles rolled by until, at last, as they crested the final hilltop and saw the Mile High City, surrounded by towering snow peaks, sparkling below them, Pete thrust his hand right up into her crotch.

She shrieked, grabbing his arm to push him away. But he was stronger, forcing his hand between her legs, running his finger up the seam of her jeans.

"Hey!" she cried, dead serious. "Pete! Stop!" She was digging her nails into his biceps, trying to wriggle away from him.

"Big strong girlie-girl," Pete taunted, dropping into his false, booming bass. "You want me to stop? Do ya? I don't think so. You like it. You know it." He was putting his whole weight into it, at once pressing her down, holding her in place, and nearly lifting her out of her seat. "Pretty little sweet stuff. Better get used to it."

The car veered suddenly into the oncoming lane, so Pete swerved back and overshot, running onto the shoulder, his whole hot hand still cradling her crotch. And with the car careening over the dividing line and back again, she didn't move, she didn't dare. Besides, she told herself, she'd already let him put his hands on her for so many hundreds of miles. How could she make him stop now? By now it was a joke. If that was how she felt about it, she should have said something way back. She should have jumped out of the car in Hot Springs when he first touched her knee. She should have left her suitcase behind and hitchhiked to Denver, or knocked on a stranger's door and told them that it was an emergency, that she needed to use their phone to call her mom. She could have done that. But then she would have had to explain to Eve why she was stranded, and Eve would have had to drive all the way out there and come get her, like it or not.

"What?" she could hear Eve shouting. *"Where* are you? He touched your *knee?* Was it by accident?"

Still. There were so many things she could have done, and she hadn't done one of them. And now it was too late. They were almost to Denver—just a few more miles to go.

Pete was giddy, grinning like a cat, running his fingers over her crotch seam. And what did he mean by it? Did he like her? Did he want to be her boyfriend?

"You're pretty cool, Candy Striper," he said, bobbing his head to the radio like nothing at all was happening. "Might just hafta keep ya."

She sat rigid, looking straight ahead, her stomach in knots, wondering how much Eve actually knew about this "grandson," Pete.

Though Eve was nice to her, Pete's white-haired grandma—with her plaster-jewel brooches and over-sprayed bouffant hairdos—was "the biggest loudmouth pain in the ass in the whole bridge club," she always said. "I wish she'd quit! I'm guessing that grandson of hers only shows up to take her money. She's always bragging about leaving him with a pocketful of cash. Well, that'd be a good incentive."

But Eve was like that—always helping out old ladies and "friends" she disliked. Like when she answered the phone with her voice two octaves higher than normal, then chirped on to someone who just moments before she'd called a "flaming idiot." Which was puzzling. René could only assume that Eve liked and trusted all the people she said she didn't. But maybe she didn't like or trust any of the people she pretended to— Pete's grandma being one of them.

They finally pulled up to the Babbitts', where, René noted with relief, Pete didn't try to kiss her. He just stopped the car, pressed his full hand hard into her crotch, and said, "There ya go, babe."

Candy Striper? Sweet Stuff? Babe? Maybe he couldn't remember her name.

She got out and took her suitcase from the backseat.

"Thanks for the ride," she said through the rolled-down window of the passenger door, now firmly closed between them.

Pete extended his open hand—the same hand that had just been up between her legs.

After a momentary confusion, René said, "Oh, I almost forgot." And she reached into her jeans pocket and handed him the ten-dollar bill Eve had given her for gas.

Pete snatched it away, winked at her through the open window, then tore off, honking, leaving her standing on the broken sidewalk with her suitcase, her legs trembling beneath her—from what, she couldn't really say, because nothing had really happened, she told herself. Nothing serious. She was all in one piece, after all. She was in Denver. Delivered. As promised.

She just needed to shake it off. She needed to enter this new place clear-eyed and ready, not quivering, not falling apart—which, it seemed, was imminent, tears of anger, confusion, helplessness now way too close to the surface.

She turned to haul her suitcase up the crumbling cement steps to the Babbitts' decrepit little yellow house in the middle of the block of old, similar-looking houses, feeling that she'd somehow stumbled through an unseen doorway and wound up on the wrong side of her own life.

And suddenly, as if to confirm the notion, the scarecrow mom came dancing frantically out onto the front porch, sing-hollering, *"Helloooo theeeeeerre. We've been waaaaaiting for youuuuu,"* her spooky daughter standing quietly behind her in the doorway like a spirit, shivering and mute, seeming to brim over with eerie, unexplainable anticipation.

31

THE BEDROOM ACROSS THE HALL FROM THE SCAREcrow mom and her dying father was filled all night with the old man's coughing, spitting, yelling, and bell ringing, followed by scurrying footsteps. Often in the mornings René could see that not only had Mrs. Babbitt not slept, but that she'd been crying. Her eyes were swollen and red beneath her big glasses, and her singsong voice was no disguise.

René wasn't sleeping, either. With all the noise from the old man's room—along with the mewing of cats and the whistling of birds—she was up, tossing and turning under the filthy bedcovers, causing the canopy above her to send down dust motes like late winter snowflakes. She watched as they swirled in the strip of light shining in from the alleyway, then covered her face and tried not to breathe.

At Dicker's studio, Mrs. Babbitt was in class every night, just like Dicker had promised, sweating through her headscarf, working her exhausted body into a lather. And there were other adults in class, too—grown men who looked like they might have stepped in right off the street but who could keep up in general, even if their feet tended to flop at the ends of their legs like canoes in a storm. Mostly there was a lot of stumbling and hopping about, but Dicker didn't seem to mind. He wore his three-piece suit and shiny loafers instead of tights and ballet slippers, and presided over the class like a monarch, preening and distracted.

He'd demonstrate combinations with exaggerated aplomb, as if he were onstage, then walk the length of the studio, checking his reflection in the mirror—smoothing his hair, straightening his vest, brandishing his shiny walking stick. Sometimes he'd stop during a barre exercise to adjust one of the grown-ups' ports de bras, or interrupt a center-floor combination to tease one of the older guys about a botched combination or a turned-in supporting leg and splayed hip, taking the time to demonstrate just how silly the guy had looked, making everyone laugh.

At least René was relieved to find that, even after all her summer indulgences, she was skinny compared to the other girls at Dicker's studio—though that didn't seem to matter here. There was a girl whose over-ample backside made her look like she was wearing jodhpurs, and another who ballooned out around the middle—extra flesh like an overflow of molten candle wax spilling over the waistband of her tights—and no one looked twice, much less made a comment.

But, for reasons she couldn't discern—admiration of her clean lines? anger about Eve's asking for a discount?—Dicker kept his distance, scanning her silently, his head tipped so far back he had to look down his nose.

So it was confusing. Like everything else in Denver, ballet was different—less exacting and ambitious, more laid-back and egalitarian. There was no struggle for rank, since no one seemed to have a position in mind. There was an older girl, Marcie, who worked at a real estate office downtown and was obviously Dicker's favorite. She'd already tried her luck in New York and—"after too many girls and too few chances," as Mrs. Babbitt told it—had simply come back and decided to stay.

And one night, after Dicker had spent an entire class praising some new guy René had never seen in class before—a guy who pirouetted on flat feet and did grand jetés across the floor like he was kicking one football after another—René realized that there was going to be nothing for her in Denver. And she began to wonder what she was doing here.

Especially since she couldn't imagine how she was going to make her way from here to where she was actually trying to go, which—though, of course, was to be a professional, a principal, a star—was still hazy, like a distant castle on a clouded hilltop, including every equivalent to a moat and a bolted gate and a hidden key. If she was ever going to dance in New York City—like Carly, Didi, Terri, and those other Phoenix girls were bound to do—she was now going to have to get there by slogging through this Denver backwater.

"Anyone can go to New York," Eve said impatiently over the phone one evening, interrupting René's latest rant about Dicker—his cavalier attitude, his shoddy, untrained students, his continuous silence. "A lot can happen between now and then, you know. First you have to finish high school. That's the main thing. And Denver's as good a place as any for that. You'll just have to try your best, René." Eve was scolding. "It's too late to go back to Phoenix now, anyway. I can't imagine Mr. B's had any better luck finding you a place—"

René cringed at the thought of Mr. B—at how kind and encouraging he'd always been, at how he'd pleaded with her to come back, warned her to listen.

And as Eve harangued on, René felt all her high hopes deserting her, as if every door she'd fought so hard to open were locking shut. With nothing in Denver to reach for, nothing to rise to, and Mr. B now out of the picture, all her chips were on Dicker. If Dicker wasn't going to help her, there wasn't going to be anybody else. It was Dicker or nobody.

"Looks like it's going to be whatever you decide to make it," Eve was saying, transitioning to one of her pep talks. "Just work hard. Do your best. You know how to do that. Then you can do whatever you want. Trust me."

But trusting Eve was beside the point. Eve didn't know. And like she'd just said—it was René's problem now.

She'd have to do her best—whatever that might mean at this second-rate dance studio where she'd landed by a collision of lack: lack of a place to stay, lack of courage, lack of information, lack of funds, lack of faith in Mr. B. Because no matter how she'd ended up here or why she had to stay—in this place where it felt like her dreams were suddenly dangling headlong over a precipice—it was clear there'd be no going back.

She was here. And there was a long way to go.

32

After Mother Mary Ignatius in Phoenix, the dryly named Denver Catholic High was more like a public school back home—groups gathering and dispersing in the hallways, cheerleaders hosting bake sales, jocks roughing one another up against lockers, couples holding hands, leaning in, whispering in corners.

At least René didn't have to wear a uniform or spend her lunchtime watching those Mother Mary Ignatius girls running in circles around the courtyard, lifting each other's skirts. And compared to the workload in Phoenix, her studies at Denver Catholic were simple—no more homework, no more essay questions, no more harsh injunctions or raised eyebrows. Here again were the familiar mimeographed worksheets, the tests where you could choose (a), (b), (c), or (d) all of the above, and be done with it. Even the graduation requirements were minimal. If she planned it right, she could condense two years into one and get out.

She took Speech and stood swaying in front of her classmates, relating facts about Mother Teresa she'd lifted from a single page of the encyclopedia. She took Family Planning with Mr. Davis, where they colored in worksheets on the reproductive parts of flowers. The class was all girls, and when they got to the part about "saving themselves" for marriage, Mr. Davis took a poll.

"Just wait," he said when almost everyone in class raised a hand to confirm their abstinence. "You're gonna change your minds."

"I'd change my mind for you, Jim!" one of the girls tipping her desk to recline against the back wall called out, making the others giggle.

Mr. Davis was young and built, solid and broad with dusty-brown hair and a chiseled jaw, obviously an athlete. He was easygoing and friendly. All the girls liked him.

Then one day her English teacher, Janet Zee—who'd told the class to call her Janet, "just Janet"—called René up to her desk to ask why she hadn't been doing the reading. Shocked that her neglect of *In Cold Blood* was apparent, René ended up telling Janet about being away from home, about living with a family she didn't know, about dancing, about trying not to eat, and about her brother, Leon, who'd already been in jail twice for DUIs, how things at home always seemed unfair to him.

"It's too scary," she told her. "It's too real."

"It *is* real. That's what makes it so sad," Janet sighed.

So Janet understood, even sympathized. And after that, René started lingering at Janet's desk each day as the rest of the class cleared out.

Janet was short, with stark blond hair that feathered around her face in pretty layers, and matronly, even though she was young. She had a warm gaze that landed on you and stayed there. Whatever you might say to her, she'd give you a wry smile and roll her eyes—like you were funny, but also like she'd heard it all before.

Janet was separated and had a little daughter she was struggling to raise. She was lonely and wanted to be married again—not to her husband, who wouldn't even give her a divorce. She just wanted to find someone who wasn't a "complete asshole," she told René.

René also heard from Janet that some of the other kids in class had their own problems—like never having any lunch money, or spending too much time getting high in the parking lot instead of going to class. Because Janet got to know her students. She felt responsible for them, followed their lives and did what she could to help.

So when René finally worked up the nerve to ask Janet about Dan—the cowboy guy with the dark curly hair and big, toothy smile, who sat in the back row, and who'd recently been catching her eye as they passed in the hallways, grinning at her like he was hiding a game for them to play—she learned that he wasn't just another ranch kid but a real rodeo guy, a bronc rider.

"He's won bunches of prizes. *So* many," Janet said, widening her eyes to show that the list of medals and ribbons he likely had was way too long to catalog. "Trophies, cash purses, you name it."

Dan wore a cowboy hat and tight jeans with a shiny rodeo buckle to school, ducking his head to say hello and strutting the halls in his cowboy boots like he was leading a victory parade. Just looking at him made René feel like somewhere inside her a light had blinked on.

Janet didn't believe in tests, so she graded on discussion. And René soon found that, though Dan kept the kids around him in stitches, he didn't do much of the reading. Mainly he was an artist, he piped up to say one day as the class was going over *A Portrait of the Artist as a Young Man*. He liked to draw horses in pencil, "sometimes charcoal," he said. He hadn't said anything for a while, so he was trying to get a word in, clearly taking his cue from the title.

"I don't think he's read a single book all year," Janet lamented after class. "But he's a good kid. He's got his own thing going on."

René agreed. She was like that, too. She had her own thing going on.

"Plus he's so damn cute," Janet added, shimmying her shoulders and tossing her feathery blond hair, smiling. "What're ya gonna do?"

And later that afternoon, as they passed in the hall, René swung around to look back at Dan—struck by his long sturdy frame, by how easily he might be leaning up close to her at her locker as she soaked in his deep, rich ranch smell—and found that he'd turned, too, and was blushing and thumbing his hat the way cowboys did in the movies when they caught sight of a girl they liked in a saloon.

After that, she was watching for Dan everywhere.

33

DAYS AND WEEKS WENT BY WITH NOTHING MUCH happening at Dicker's. There was class every night but Dicker didn't have anything to say—only that René should lower her shoulders or pull in her thumbs.

Though she was still trying not to eat, she found herself careening back and forth between starvation and gluttony. Mainly, she'd have dry salad and a hard-boiled egg in the school cafeteria. But when there was cornbread floating in maple syrup, she convinced herself it was time for a treat, and when it was taco day, she figured there wasn't much difference between an egg and a spoonful of hamburger, and she went ahead.

"All shapes and sizes of people love to dance, you know," Mrs. Babbitt said one day, setting out a plate of Hydrox cookies. "No one should feel like they have to fit into someone else's mold." She did a wobbly tour de basque, catching herself on the kitchen counter, and tilted her head, causing her glasses to slip.

"Sure," René said, thinking, *Sure, if you want to dance around the kitchen, or barefoot in the grass at a park somewhere. But classical ballet? In New York City?*

No matter what kind of world Mrs. Babbitt might dream of or wish for, it didn't work that way.

Kat suggested René try sticking a finger down her throat and throwing up. "You could eat whatever you wanted," she chirped, shrugging.

So the next night, after Mrs. Babbitt had stopped for burritos on their way home from ballet, René dug in, loading up on sour cream and salsa. And later, she bent over the toilet, crammed a finger down her throat, and made all the right noises. But no luck.

Then Mrs. Babbitt said she should try eating before ballet class. "Not that you need to, but you'd burn up all those calories. Presto!" She snapped her fingers above her head like a flamenco dancer as Kat nodded behind her.

But with nothing to win or lose in Denver—with no more calorie notebooks to keep, no more logging her weight each night—René found that Mrs. Babbitt had a point. There was no real need to restrain her appetite or deny her desires. She didn't have to be that same girl she'd been in Phoenix. She could be different. Here, in Denver, she could be herself. And if only she could get back to the happier, sweeter, more carefree parts of herself—*the real parts,* she thought—then maybe Dan would like her.

Because what she could see most clearly—from the kids holding hands at school, from the silent, despairing aloneness of Mrs. Babbitt, which she attempted to cover with wan smiles and awkward melodies, from Janet's open sadness—was how comforting it would be to simply belong to someone.

She could remember Eve and Mrs. G chuckling uneasily about boys, about how they always ended up ruining a girl's life: "If it wasn't for Doug showing up in the middle of my dance career and getting me pregnant," Mrs. G would start, grinning and shaking her head.

"You don't have to tell *me*," Eve would say, tsking. "I know that story—just *all too well*."

"You'd never do anything as stupid as all that, would you?" Mrs. G would say, putting her hand on René's head.

"No," René would answer proudly each time, as Eve snorted and rolled her eyes and Mrs. G laughed along.

How old had she been back then? *Nine? Maybe ten?*

Still, it didn't have to be like that. She could be Dan's girl. Why not? It wasn't too much to ask, was it? To have that simple piece of a normal life?

34

Each morning she bundled up, got on the number 23 bus, took a transfer, then got off at Saint Joseph Hospital, where she waited, craning her neck, crumpling the transfer in her pocket until the number 20 finally showed up to take her to school. It was cold—the skies gray and heavy with clouds, the air biting, thick with the promise of snow. And as she watched for the number 20, her breath crystallizing in front of her, René would find herself gazing down the road, mesmerized by the gleaming windows of Saint Joseph, thinking how lucky all those people were in their warm hospital beds, sleeping until noon, pushing a button to sit up or lie down, nurses bringing whatever they wanted—warm blankets, cups of fruit cocktail.

What she wouldn't give to spend a few days in one of those hospital beds with people looking after her. What she wouldn't give to be in Saint Joseph instead of at this frozen bus stop, or across the hall from the Babbitts' old grandpa, or at what she'd come to think of as Dicker's little ballet club.

Until one day—hiding her hands up her sleeves, stamping her feet on the icy pavement, waiting for the number 20—she saw Dan whiz past in a beat-up pickup, his little brother in the cab with him.

She waved, but too late. He was gone.

After that, she watched for him every morning, figuring that once he saw her standing out in the cold like that, he'd stop and pick her up. They were going to the same place anyway, and there was plenty of room for three in the cab. So she took to waving as soon as she spotted his truck. And when he finally caught sight of her, he waved back.

From then on Dan waved and René waved and Dan honked his horn. But he didn't stop. Not once. Even when the snow was flying and René was folded in on herself—snowflakes settling on her back and shoulders as she stood shivering—Dan flew past in his pickup, smiling and honking.

And as soon as he was out of sight, her mind would drift back to the hospital, dreaming of how nice it would be to be in there, thinking over and over how if only she could be in there, with all those people taking care of her, she could finally go back to being the carefree, self-assured, lighthearted girl she used to be—the girl who'd walked barefoot in the woods, collecting quartz, who'd climbed high into a tree house to look out over the distant hills for beaver dams and deer trails, wondering where Leon had gone until she heard him in the distance crying, "Timber!" as he felled yet another young sapling—the girl who'd never once given a thought to not being thin enough or good enough, or to raising anyone up.

35

With no ride home for Thanksgiving, René stayed in Denver and got to meet Mrs. Babbitt's older daughter, Deborah.

"We keep her room for her in the basement," Mrs. Babbitt admitted, smiling, happy to be talking about her eldest daughter. "We might have offered it to you, but we're under strict orders, aren't we, Kittykat?"

Kat stood across the kitchen, grinning and bobbing her head.

It turned out there was an enormous beautiful room in the Babbitts' basement that, despite the exposed concrete walls, was clean and brightly decorated, with a white shag area rug, a flowered duvet, framed Lichtenstein and Warhol posters, and perfectly organized bookshelves. But it was clearly off-limits. Though Deborah was currently "sharing an apartment with a married man," as Mrs. Babbitt explained, she insisted her room be kept vacant. Likely for when the man had to spend a few nights with his wife, René figured, though Mrs. Babbitt didn't say.

"'No humans and no animals!'" Mrs. Babbitt said, quoting her older daughter. "She has her own ways." She gave René a crooked smile.

And just then the front door flew open and in walked Deborah, her arms full of flowers, a small jug of apple cider hanging by two fingers.

Though Kat's older sister talked and joked easily with her family, what she brought to mind most was the misfit daughter from *The Munsters*. There was nothing about her that wasn't perfectly normal, even beautiful. She wore a crisp white shirt with a high ruffled collar and dark flared pants with a skinny patent leather belt, and she was slender, with deep blue eyes that twinkled when she laughed and natural blond hair that fell in careful waves to just below her shoulders.

Of course, they all revered her. Mrs. Babbitt bent to Deborah's wishes in anticipation of any request. And Kat simply adored her. Which was easy, René figured, because, inside and out, she was lovely.

The only mystery was what she was doing living with a married man. But that didn't seem to be anybody's business. Because, unlike at René's house—where it would have been the very center of Thanksgiving, the sun around which everyone and everything revolved—at the Babbitts', it wasn't spoken of. And not only did no one mention it, no one really seemed to care. They were just happy for her company.

Because, like Eve had first said—above all, the Babbitts were kind. The only thing they wanted from this daughter, this sister—the only thing they cared about—was *her*, however she came to them. Her presence, her nearness, her very existence was fulfillment, and enough.

"*Looks like we're readyyyy*—" Mrs. Babbitt sang, taking the turkey breast out of the oven, then tilting her head and spreading her arms over her head like a child miming a sunrise.

Kat got out plates and Deborah sliced bread and put out cheeses and cups of cider, while the cats meowed, prowling the kitchen, jumping up onto the counters to sniff at dishes and lap up spills. But instead of shooing them away—knocking them to the floor or even tossing them outside, like Eve would have done—the Babbitts simply stroked their fur, kissed their heads, and talked to them in baby talk.

So, after shaking out the placemats, setting the overflowing basket of junk mail on top of the refrigerator, then clearing the parakeet food and cat toys, the four of them crowded around the Babbitts' small kitchen table to share Thanksgiving.

Mrs. Babbitt was no cook, and the Babbitts' Thanksgiving was a mere sketch of the holiday—a dried-up turkey breast, boxed potatoes, canned gravy, frozen green beans, bread, cider, along with an avocado half on each plate, the seed pocket filled with half mayonnaise and half ketchup, each in its own red or white pool.

"The colors of the Italian flag," Mrs. Babbitt said to René. "A family tradition. To the arts!" she toasted, raising her avocado.

The girls raised theirs, too.

"Opera!" Mrs. Babbitt called.

"Ballet!" Kat countered.

"Ballet!" René chimed in, and they all laughed.

"All that—" Deborah said, laughing, holding her avocado up with the others. "And family, too."

They smiled, Mrs. Babbitt's cheeks going bright pink. Then they dug in.

36

ONE NIGHT AFTER SCHOOL HAD STARTED AGAIN and they were all home from dance class, Mrs. Babbitt called down the hall in her singsong to say that René had a phone call.

"A boy!" she chimed, covering the receiver, raising her eyebrows.

It was Dan, out of the blue.

He wondered if she wanted to go out, "like to a restaurant or somethin'."

"Sure," she said, her heart jumping as Mrs. Babbitt scurried, humming, out of the kitchen.

"And, hey—maybe I can give you a ride to school sometime."

"That'd be great," she said, trying to make it sound like it was nothing to her one way or the other.

Still, the next day and the day after that, Dan drove right past her, honking and waving, even making his pickup backfire, which sent his little brother into hysterics. So when their date night finally arrived and Dan pulled up to the Babbitts' in a long tan Buick, then came to the door wearing a brown western blazer with decorative stitching, a white button-down cowboy shirt with black piping, and a bolo tie with a smooth turquoise stone, René was just glad he'd remembered.

Dan stepped inside and, nervously holding his keys in both hands, said hello to Mrs. Babbitt and Kat, then bent to pet the cats, who were rubbing against his legs, leaving cat hair all over his clean, pressed pants as René stood smiling, cringing. Though René had finally adjusted to the Babbitts—to the cats and birds, to the awkward strangeness of Kat and her scarecrow mom, including their goofy matching eyeglasses—she knew what it must look like to Dan. And, once again aware of the dusty lamps and dirty birdcages, the mixed-up odors of urine and decay, she wanted to say, *This isn't my house! My house isn't anything like this!* But she stood, mute—recalling the shining windows that looked out onto the wide green lawn back home, the polished furniture, the air filled with the smell of Eve's baking.

"I'm ready!" she said abruptly.

Dan smiled and opened the screen door, holding it for her.

"Nice to meet you," he called back, raising a hand to the Babbitts as Kat grinned from behind the kitchen archway and Mrs. Babbitt leaned on the piano at such an angle that it looked as if, on letting go, she'd keel over sideways.

Dan took her to a country club his parents belonged to. He ordered White Russians, laughing nervously when the waiter turned away, saying he hoped the guy didn't come back for IDs. René told him about her dad being a cattle dealer, about leaving home to study ballet, and he told her about his folks on the ranch, having to get up early for chores, about his favorite horses and how he liked to draw western scenes. By the time the waiter came around with dessert, they were holding hands under the table.

"I can make you a drawing if you want." Dan was leaning close, nearly whispering. "You can take it home for your dad when you go for Christmas. I don't know if he'd like it."

"He would. He'd love it," René said, thinking of how Al always pointed out the framed Remington western prints when she went with him to the bank, imagining how pleased he'd be.

She sat next to Dan on the ride home. They held hands as he drove—slowly, as though he couldn't bear to drop her off. When they got to the Babbitts', he killed the engine and put his arm around her.

And thinking how they were going to have a lot more nights like this one—since they talked so easily and had so much in common—René went through the calculus of kissing a boy on the first date. It wasn't that she'd never kissed a boy before. Back in junior high she'd kissed Tom and those other boys in that tent they'd set up in the field across from the church. Sure, they'd dared her, but that didn't mean she hadn't wanted to. But this was different. This was Dan, with his arm around her, leaning in.

And taking her cue from his good manners, she pulled back. Because first she needed him to know that she wasn't just anybody, certainly not a girl *like that.*

"I'd better go. It's pretty late," she heard herself saying.

Dan sat back, clearly surprised and disappointed.

"Thanks for the nice night," she went on, her voice tinny

and false. Even as she said it she regretted it, wishing for a way to turn it around.

She leaned over and gave him a quick kiss on the cheek, like they were playing a game of fancy lady tea party. Then she got out of the car.

Dan got out, too. He came around and took her hand without saying a word. He walked her to the bottom of the Babbitts' crumbling steps and waited as she went in.

Once inside, René ran back to the filthy bedroom across the hall from Mrs. Babbitt's dying father and lay down under the dusty canopy nearly in tears, reeling from both the beautiful kiss that hadn't happened and this new landscape now rising in front of her. Because there was something in the way Dan had looked at her—at the door, in the car, across the table at the restaurant—how he'd *seen* her there, how he'd *wanted* her there.

It was unfamiliar and confusing, pointing as it did to the possibility of happiness without suffering—without accomplishment or achievement or success or the ability to endure and carry on, without anything at all attached to it or sacrificed for it—just simple happiness at each other's company. It took her breath away.

She liked him. He liked her.

And, somehow—like magic—that was enough.

At school the next day Dan said hi to her in the hallway, giving her a wink, but he stuck with his group. Still, when she turned to take in his long perfect frame, to follow his high swagger, she found his cowboy buddies laughing and elbowing him, shoving him lightly down the hall.

He called her again the next week to tell her that the drawing he was making for her dad was almost finished. He'd give it to her at school, he said. And a few days after that, he broke away from his friends and came right up to her.

"I rolled it so you can take it home easier," he said, handing her a cardboard tube. "It didn't come out just right, but I thought I better get it to you before you leave."

There were only a few days left before Christmas break.

"I hope your dad likes it. I wanted it to be just right, but it didn't exactly come out." He pushed his hat back.

"I'm sure it's great."

She was aching to tell him how she'd wanted to kiss him that night, how she wished she'd moved closer instead of pulling away, that she wanted to kiss him even right now, standing here in the hallway. She didn't understand how so many days could have gone by without a chance to make it right, she wanted to say. If only he'd called her again and asked her out, she'd have kissed him as much as he wanted.

"All right," Dan was saying. "But if he doesn't like it, I can make him another one."

"Okay. But he's going to love it. Promise."

"Well. Merry Christmas." Dan was suddenly shy, shrugging, ducking his head as he started to turn away. "See you when you get back."

"Here." René quickly took hold of the single notebook he was carrying, folded it open, and began to write on the inside. "My number at home. In case you want to call."

Dan smiled, nodding and blushing. Then he turned to rejoin his friends, bounding down the hallway like a kid goat in a spring meadow.

I'll kiss him, she told herself, giddy. *I'll kiss him the first chance I get, as soon as I get back.*

RAPID CITY, 1974

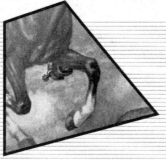

The Visitation

37

"It's not exactly how we planned it, now is it?" Eve said when she and Jayne picked René up at the airport. Because there hadn't been a ride home for René at Christmas, either. She'd had to fly.

"All these goddamn plane fares," Eve went on, shaking her head.

It wasn't the welcome René had expected.

"I guess you'll just have to take your grandmother's car when you go back."

"That's what we first talked about, isn't it? Remember?"

"Not for driving around town, you understand. Just for coming back and forth."

"But I can take it to school, right?"

"I don't see how that's necessary."

When they were all in the car Eve lit a cigarette. She pulled onto the two-lane from the airport, and they drove through Rapid Valley, past the speedway, familiar frozen pastures on both sides, the peaks of the Black Hills carving jagged lines in the distance.

"I have to take it to school," René repeated. "Why would I even have it if I can't take it to school?"

"We'll see." Eve cracked her window and looked away, blowing smoke.

René had just arrived and already she could tell that, whatever Eve had been doing before coming to the airport—cooking, cleaning, sewing, laundry, making beds—picking up René was "the last straw."

Still, walking in through the back door, she was blanketed with the smell of cinnamon, nutmeg, cloves—Eve's baking for the holidays. She headed straight for the Christmas cookies—frosted and stacked in standing rows in the kitchen—and took a deep breath.

"Well, hello there!" Al called out from the next room. "Just in time! I'm going to need some extra hands. What d'you say?"

"I'll help," Jayne called back, taking René by the arm and pulling her along into the breakfast nook, where Al was kneading candy cream on a marble board. It had to be worked like taffy until it changed from a dull, grainy paste to a smooth, glossy fondant. Stop, and it turned to brick.

"Well, hi there, honey," Al said, looking up, smiling. "Will you look at that. Here you are. Now we know it's really Christmas." He laughed, delighted, and Jayne and René laughed with him.

It really was. It was Christmas. There were fruitcakes lining the kitchen counters, homemade caramels wrapped in waxed paper, stacked in a heap on the sideboard, holiday tins filled with peanut brittle, ready to hand out to neighbors, miniature mountains of divinity fudge and caramel corn—

Eve's annual handiwork. Al was home, working on Christmas candy, rounding up helpers, while Eve rustled pots and pans in the kitchen.

"Is Leon coming home?" René asked.

The question landed like a stone and was followed by a deep, reverberating silence—Al suddenly dark and brooding. It took a few beats for him to recover.

"Well, now. That's a good question. I say," he said. "Eve, do you know anything about that?"

"No idea," Eve called back sharply, ending it.

"Just have to wait and see, I guess. Wait—and—see," Al repeated, putting extra muscle into his kneading.

Wherever Leon was, it could be assumed he was still drinking. The last René had heard he'd joined the navy to get out of doing more jail time. If he was still in the navy, she figured, maybe he'd get time off for Christmas. But it seemed like the less said, the better.

"Looks like we're ready," Al said as the candy cream began to glisten. "Jayne! The toothpicks!"

Jayne zipped off to the kitchen and came back with a box of toothpicks and a bowl of pecan halves. Eve came in a minute later with a trivet and a double boiler full of melted chocolate. They all knew what to do next. They were going to spend the afternoon making opera creams—rolling the fondant into balls, dipping each one into gleaming dark chocolate, dropping it onto waxed paper, and pressing a pecan half on top. It was the family Christmas candy, made every year since before any of them could remember.

On the morning of Christmas Eve, René wrapped Dan's drawing. She'd unrolled it as soon as she'd got home from school, back when he'd first handed it to her, and found an exquisitely detailed charcoal rendering of an old-time Indian on horseback—the shirtless rider slumped forward, head lowered in defeat, a great feathered staff at his side, the horse rearing back, seeming to struggle against fate itself.

Just as she was setting it under the tree, the phone rang. She picked it up, thinking maybe it was Dan—on Christmas Eve!—thinking how romantic, how serendipitous that would be.

It was Leon.

"René!" he said, shouting through the phone line. "I didn't know you'd be home. Well, I wasn't sure, anyway, but I hoped so 'cause I'm comin' home, too! Yeah. But hey, hey—keep it cool. I want it to be a surprise, so don't tell anybody, okay?"

"Everybody's going to be *so* surprised," she said quietly. And suddenly, for no reason at all, she felt herself begin to tremble.

"I know!" Leon laughed. "I'm comin' in today, kinda last minute. Can you sneak away, come get me at the airport? I think I get in around two or somethin', let me check."

There was a long pause and a scrambling on the other end—laughing and talking, swearing and shuffling of papers.

"Oh, and I'm bringin' somebody," Leon said. "A friend." He laughed, and René heard a girl correcting him in the background. "Okay, okay. A *real good* friend. Okay?"

"More like it," René heard the girl say.

"Just don't tell anybody."

"I won't."

"Thanks, René. Okay. Yup. See ya—two o'clock! Woohoo!"

They hung up and René stood frozen. It was good that Leon was coming home, but it sounded like he'd been drinking. Plus Eve and Al were definitely going to be upset about the girl, who was likely someone Leon had picked up somewhere—if the past was any measure, in a bar, last night or the night before.

René wandered silently through the house. Jayne was at the neighbor's, Al was nowhere in sight, Eve was down in the basement, frantically working to finish what she could of the gifts they'd all find wrapped under the tree in the morning—handmade polyester underwear, patchwork vests of leftover fabrics, felted slippers—all generally unwearable. By the time Eve finally gave up and decided to simply wrap the unfinished projects, then made dinner, indulging in a glass of wine, she'd have a headache. Unnerved and exhausted, she'd throw up, then go to bed. That would be Christmas Eve.

Though maybe this time would be different. Maybe there'd be real presents under the tree, maybe Leon wasn't drinking after all, maybe he was bringing home a nice girl, and maybe even Al would be happy to see him, happy to meet his girl.

René called down to say she needed to take the car to pick up one more gift she forgot about.

"All right," Eve called back, clearly agitated and distracted, her mouth full of straight pins. "Just don't be too long."

38

WHEN SHE FIRST SPOTTED LEON COMING through the doors off the snowy tarmac, he already had his arms open wide, ready for a bear hug. He was big, well over six feet, and once he got close, René could tell he was crocked. He reeked of alcohol, as if he'd spilled a bottle of Jim Beam down his shirtfront.

"I'm so glad you got off for Christmas," she said as they separated. "That's so lucky."

"Jesus, René." Leon stepped back unsteadily. "It's the navy. Goddamn. You don't get off for Christmas. Christ. You don't hardly get off to take a dump." He laughed, and the girl coming up behind him laughed, too. "Oh, I almost forgot—"

The girl—who was older, a grown-up woman—gave him a shove.

"Well, shit, lady," he said, swinging his arm around her neck. "Do I know you?"

"Lee-on!" She pounded on his jacket.

"René," Leon said, serious now, dipping his head in a wobbly bow. "This is Sally. A real special lady. Sally," he said, turning to indicate René with an exaggerated, courtly gesture, a remnant of his ballet days as a kid, "this is my sister René."

"Hi ya there, *giirl*," the lady said, obviously Leon's equal in terms of inebriation. "Nice to meet ya. Lee-on, here, just talks about ya *all the time.* God."

"In a nice way, tell her."

"In a nice way," the lady said. "And that's what I mean, baby. O' course. Nothin' but."

Sally was short and dumpy, her mop of brown hair frizzed into a perm, her raggedy macramé sweater torn and unraveling at the neckline.

Leon leaned down and gave her a sloppy kiss.

"Well. Merry Christmas. This's gonna be fun," he said, straightening up, laughing, sounding more nervous than sure.

They started for the car.

"You're gonna love the house," Leon was saying to Sally. "And we're just gonna have to hope the folks are in a good mood. Right, René?"

"Right," René said, thinking that if anything Leon had in mind was a pipe dream, it was that—or would be, after his arrival, drunk and hauling drunk Sally behind him.

As they approached the corner of Fifth and St. Pat, Leon poked René in the leg, telling her to pull into the liquor store.

"I've been gone too long already," she tried. "They're going to know something's up."

"Just stop. Stop the car, René. Right now. Pull over! I mean it," Leon ordered, getting edgy. "Stop the car or I'm gonna knock you outta that driver's seat and take over myself."

When Leon was drinking, he could turn on a dime.

She pulled into the parking lot.

"I gotta get Dad a little gift," he said, as if nothing at all had just happened, as if everything was just the same. "Come on."

So they all piled out of the car and went into the liquor store, where Leon and Sally cruised the aisles while René followed, the man behind the cash register watching their every move.

Leon finally picked out a Kahlúa gift set for Al—a big bottle of liqueur boxed with an enormous plastic Aztec mug.

"Everybody likes Kahlúa," he said as he got out his money, the cashier keeping his eye on both Leon and Sally, who was running her hand over the tequila bottles near the register like she was petting a cat.

39

By the time they pulled into the driveway, everyone was home.

Leon stepped in through the back door with Sally in tow, and René could see Al—who was at the top of the back steps, on his way to the kitchen—totter and grab for the stair rail.

"Well. My word," Al said. "Isn't this a surprise. It sure is." Then he called out, as if for reinforcements, "Eve! I think you'd better come on up here."

"Hi, Dad," Leon said.

"Well, hi there, Leon. I didn't know we were expecting you."

"Kinda last minute," Leon said. "Just wanted to surprise ya."

"Well, you've done that much, all right," Al confirmed. "That you have done. Come on in."

Al moved away, turning into the kitchen as Eve bounded up the basement steps screaming, "Leon! Leon! We didn't know you were coming! So good to see you, honey. Come in. Come in. Come on."

"Mom." Leon stopped her. "This here's Sally, a friend of mine."

Eve shook Sally's hand and gave Leon a big hug. "Come in, you two," she said. "Let's get you something to eat." She led them up through the kitchen and into the breakfast room, where Al was sitting, looking out the window, lighting up a cigarette. "Here," she said. "You sit and talk and I'll get you something. There's lots of treats around. Too many! Help yourself to anything."

"This's Sally," Leon said to Al as they sat down.

Then Jayne ran into the room and hugged Leon around the neck.

"Hey, there," Leon said, and Jayne stayed with him, standing behind his chair.

"Sally, this is my dad, and my little sister Jayne."

"Hi," Jayne said, waving. Sally waved back wildly, and Jayne moved to stand next to René in the doorway, taking René's arm and putting it over her shoulder, holding on to her hand.

"Well, now. How do you do, there, Sally?" Al said, barely raising his eyes.

"Good, thanks," Sally said. "Nice to meet ya. I heard a lot about ya."

Al surveyed her out of the corner of his eye through a haze of new cigarette smoke. "Well, I imagine you have. That I do," he said soberly, dropping his head, tapping his cigarette onto an empty plate.

It was quiet for a minute. Then Leon picked up the liquor store bag he'd placed at his feet.

"Here, Dad. I bought you somethin'. For Christmas. You

might as well just have it." He laughed nervously, looking over to Sally. "Close enough, right?"

So Al took the brown paper bag from Leon and lifted out the Kahlúa gift set.

"Will you look at that," he said, deadpan. "What in the world?" He turned to Jayne and René as if for an explanation, then turned back. "Now, what am I supposed to do with something like that?"

"It's good," Leon started. "Everybody likes it—in coffee, on top of ice cream, with milk, like a milkshake. Straight up. On ice." He laughed, likely at all the options he was able to come up with. "I think you'll like it, Dad. Just try it sometime. I don't know." Leon shrugged, giving up.

"Doesn't really look like it's for me, is all," Al said, narrowing his eyes and looking from Leon to Sally and back again. "Looks like it might be for you two."

"You don't have to try it," Leon said. "Doesn't matter. Maybe Mom'll want some."

"I'm guessing she will," Al said. "That sounds about right."

"I didn't know what to get ya," Leon said, defeated.

"Well, this is just right, then. Just dandy. We'll use that up. No doubt." There was only a slight pause before Al went on. "And where might you two be planning on staying tonight? I imagine you've got some plans."

"Jesus. Never mind, Dad. We're good. Yeah." Leon started to get up, heavily, in a kind of uneven slow motion, looking at Sally, shaking his head. "We're all good."

Then Eve came into the room balancing two cups of coffee and two cinnamon rolls. "Sit down, Leon," she said. "Sit. I warmed this up just for you."

Leon sat back down, smiling again, suddenly lit up. "These are my mom's famous caramel rolls," he said to Sally. "Take a bite, one bite. I'm tellin' ya. You never tasted anything so good."

"So." Eve sat at the table with them, reaching to take Leon's hand. "How's everything, Leon? How's everything going? How's the navy treating you? You must be off for the holidays. It's so nice you came home. We're all so happy to see you, Leon. Isn't that right, Al."

Al nodded, lowering his eyes and bobbing his head like he was trying to figure out an impossible mathematical equation.

"I'm so glad you're here," Eve repeated. "I've been thinking about you so much lately."

"Yeah. It's good to be home," Leon said. He turned to Sally with his mouth full. "Wow. Didn't I tell ya? Didn't I tell ya? What'd I tell ya? Right?"

Sally nodded and giggled, her mouth full, too.

"I'll get some rooms ready for you," Eve said. "The girls can share. That's fun for Christmas." She glanced at René and Jayne, who were still standing together in the kitchen doorway. "I'll get a bed ready for you, Leon, and one for Sally."

Al stood up, pushed his chair back, and walked right out of the room.

"Don't you worry about a thing," Eve went on. "I'll get it all set."

They listened as the back door slammed. They heard Al's car start, heard him pulling out of the driveway and heading down the block.

"I do have something to tell you, though, Mom," Leon started cautiously, once he'd given enough time to make sure

Al was really gone. "Just so you know—" He stopped, drawing it out as Eve leaned back. "I'm not in the navy anymore. I left. I had to. It wasn't the place for me, Mom. No way. I mean—I could tell ya stories. You bet. Like this one new guy? They threw him overboard in the middle of the night. *No shit.* Happened right in front of me. Honest to God. But it was so dark I couldn't see nothin'. Just heard some whisperin' and saw this buncha guys strugglin' on deck, then *splash*! No siren, no 'Man overboard!' Nothin'."

Leon was moving his arms as he talked, re-creating the scene in pantomime.

"Then no more new guy. Like he'd never been there. And no report. I even looked for it the next day and the day after that. Nothin'. But I had to keep my mouth shut. Who knows who might be in on it, right? Gotta be smart about these things. Jesus. And there's more like that. Lots more. Scary shit I can't even repeat."

Leon shook his head, looking down at the table. Both he and Sally seemed to be sobering up, as if the weight of the moment was grounding them, likely with help from the coffee and rolls.

"Anyways, I left. I had to," Leon said. "I had enough."

"But, Leon." Eve finally leaned forward. "What are you going to do now? How are you going to live? How are you going to get by?"

"I dunno, Mom. That's just it. I don't know. I might need to ask for a loan. Just to get started. I'll pay ya back. 'Course I will."

"Tell me you at least got an honorable discharge, Leon. Tell me that much."

Leon stared long and hard into his empty coffee cup and didn't answer.

"Oh, Leon," Eve groaned. "Well—" She sighed and got up from the table to refill their coffees. "I'll go make up the beds," she said wearily. "You probably want to lie down."

"Not really. I'm not tired. But can we borrow the car? There's some friends in town I'd really like to see while I'm here. And I can't really stay that long."

"Oh, Leon," Eve said again. "You're in no shape— And after all you've been through with that already? Don't ask me. You'll have to ask your dad when he gets back."

"Never mind," Leon said. "I'll just call Fred. Fred'll come get us."

Fred was Leon's drug buddy from back in high school.

"Don't do that," Eve tried. "Just stay awhile, Leon. Stay around. Looks like what you need most is a good rest. You and Sally both."

But Leon went out to the hallway and got on the phone, so Eve cleared the dishes—telling Sally to help herself to whatever she wanted—then headed back down to the basement to finish her work. René could hear her down there running seams in a fury and swearing to herself as Leon and Sally tramped around in the kitchen, rummaging through the cupboards, opening and closing the refrigerator.

And before long there was a car in the driveway blasting its horn.

"Fred's here, Mom!" Leon yelled down. "Just wanna say bye. We'll be gone for a while. Don't wait up."

"Okay," Eve said, coming to the bottom of the steps, looking up at Leon, the perspective making him larger than life.

"You be good, Leon. Take care of yourself. And come on home tonight, remember."

"Sure," Leon laughed. "Tell Dad I say bye. His car's still gone, so—"

Eve nodded.

"Let's go," Leon called to Sally, and the two of them left by the back door.

"Bye, Leon!" René and Jayne hollered, banging on the kitchen window as they watched him slipping across the icy driveway.

"Merry Christmas!" Leon hollered back, raising a hand and smiling as he opened the passenger door, Fred, behind the wheel, raising a hand, too.

40

THE NEXT MORNING JAYNE GOT UP EARLY, WOKE René, and, passing Leon's empty bedroom, they hurried downstairs to separate gifts, to count and see who'd got the most. Eve came down, too. She turned on the oven to warm up the rolls. Al was already sitting in the breakfast nook in his pajamas, looking like he'd been there all night, chain-smoking and drinking coffee.

"Come on," Eve said to him. "The girls are ready to open presents."

"All rightie, then," Al said. And he stubbed out his cigarette, got up, and went into the bathroom.

When Al finally came out and sat in his chair, René could see that both he and Eve were angry and exhausted, bleary-eyed. No doubt they'd been fighting all night, debating the finer points of who was at fault for Leon's going AWOL, showing up drunk, ending up in the same dire straits he'd been in when he'd first signed on with the navy but with fewer options—with no place to live but the streets and a drunken woman hanging on his neck. Eve would have argued that they needed to make Leon feel welcome, regardless, that it was Al who'd always pushed him out, and Al would have said that Eve had always coddled Leon, that even now she was ready to baby her grown son when he showed up plastered with no notice and a drunk stranger. He would have said she'd let Leon grow up without taking any responsibility. And she would have said he'd never treated Leon fairly, never, so what did he expect—a person had to find comfort somewhere. The arguments didn't have to happen in front of René. She'd heard them so many times she could recite them by heart.

They ate cinnamon rolls and opened gifts—knitted socks and mufflers; cut and pinned cloth with a note promising a dress or shirt; a fifty-dollar Treasury bill to be kept in Al's safety-deposit box for the next ten years, until it matured; new hair clips and pajamas; a book from Grandma Emma.

After the other presents were unwrapped, René handed Al the tube from Dan, saying it was from a friend at school, a boy who wanted to send something home for him.

"My, oh my," Al said, shooting Eve a blistering look.

"He likes rodeo," René explained. "So when I told him you were a cattle dealer, he wanted to make you something."

"Isn't that nice," Al said, not sounding the least bit convinced.

He pulled out the drawing slowly, unrolled it, and held it up, looking it over as the rest of them waited, staring at the blank back of the paper.

"Do you like it?" René asked.

"Why, yes. Yes, siree. It's just fine." Al paused and inclined his head to adjust the angle of his vision. "But look at that horse's head, will you? That horse's head does not go with that body. See that?"

He turned the drawing around for everyone to see, and there again was the defeated Indian, the stricken, rearing horse.

"That horse head is just way too big. No horse I ever saw in my life had a head that big."

"I think it's very nice," Eve said, straightening her spine to oppose him. "I think it's perfect. And he's obviously talented." She looked at René.

"I never said he wasn't talented, Eve. Of course he's got talent. I never said he didn't have talent. Is that what you heard? Well, for crying out loud, I wasn't saying that, not at all."

"Sounded like it to me." Eve was more than ready to get into it.

"Well, you can put a stop to that idea right now, because I never said that. What I said, and what I *meant,* was that the horse's head—*You see? See that?*—that horse's head right there"—Al jabbed at the paper where the horse was straining upward against an inevitable loss, an outcome it had no control over—"is just way too big for its body. That's what I'm saying, and that's *all* I'm saying. And I'd appreciate you not putting words in my mouth. For crying out loud, Eve." He turned back to Dan's drawing. "All you have to do is look at it to see."

"Well, I'm looking at it," Eve said, furious, "and I think it's a fine picture."

"*Fine?* Isn't that what I said? Wasn't that the first thing I said? It *is* fine. I never said it wasn't fine. It's terrific. Absolutely fantastic! But that head, that one head is out of proportion with the rest. That's what I'm saying, and that's *all* I'm saying. That's it."

"You done, Al?"

"Why, yes, I'm done. My goodness. I was done a long time ago."

"I'll say," Eve said, and she got up and started for the kitchen with her empty plate and coffee cup. "Merry Christmas, everybody," she said caustically as she left the room, tears starting down her cheeks. And they could all hear her in the kitchen, sniffling and blowing her nose as Al sat back in his chair looking gut-punched, still holding up the drawing.

"Thank you for the gift, René," he said carefully. "And tell your friend thank you. I hope you'll tell him how much I like it." He smiled sadly.

René nodded. "I will."

Then Jayne began to quietly gather her Christmas gifts, setting them in a little pile, not even changing out of her Santa Claus pajamas before quickly heading out the door for the neighbor's house, and René followed her lead, gathering her things and taking them up to her bedroom, while Al rolled up the drawing, put it back in the tube, lit a cigarette, and turned on the television.

René fell onto her bed, listening as the TV rambled on and the smell of Eve's Christmas dinner began to fill the house.

There were only a few days left before she had to go back to Denver.

Dan hadn't called. Not on Christmas Eve, not on Christmas Day. Not once. But no matter all that had or hadn't happened here—with Leon, with Eve and Al—at least, for now, she was home, in her own room, in her own bed.

She opened her new book from Grandma Emma: "'Christmas won't be Christmas without any presents,' grumbled Jo, lying on the rug."

She sat up, picked up a pencil, and in the space between *any* and *presents,* she wrote *real*—sideways, like smoke coming out of a chimney—imagining what *real* presents from a *real* store might look like, and what it might feel like to have the *real* happiness of Christmas in your house, and in your heart, and in all the hearts of all the people you loved.

And it struck her that this new sentence she'd made might be the only sentence in the whole world that made any sense. Because Christmas hadn't been Christmas at all. Not even close.

But then, like Eve always said, nothing was ever good enough for René. Turned out, not even Christmas. She didn't have the least desire for any of the crap she'd found under the tree—extra ponytail holders from the drugstore, money she couldn't spend, unfinished, ill-fitting clothes she'd never wear.

Yet, even after everything—after the meager gifts, after the misery she always seemed to find here—she was going to miss being home. She'd be leaving in just a few days, and beyond any hope of understanding why, she was going to miss everything about it.

DENVER, 1975

Into the Wind

41

RENÉ CLUTCHED THE PIECE OF PAPER WITH EVE'S directions, crushing it against the steering wheel. She had a vague idea of how to get back to Denver, but she didn't really know the way. Plus it was snowing, lightly at first—snowflakes dancing in the air around her, disappearing as they hit the pavement—then heavier and heavier.

There were no other cars on the road, just a few stray trucks going way too fast, pushing her over to the shoulder, throwing snow and muddy slush onto her windshield, making her wipers useless. And while the day grew dimly brighter, it seemed the sun had forgotten to rise.

By the time she got to the exit at Hot Springs, the snow was deep, making the actual turnoff unclear. She could see the outline of the exit ramp by the shape of the drifts, by how they sagged and gapped. So—heart pounding, hands gripping the wheel, knowing that the slightest hesitation would be enough to send her into a ditch where she'd lie unfound for hours or days—she gunned it, leaning over the steering wheel, turning off the highway and plowing headlong into snow higher than her headlights, her wipers clapping back and forth, leaving slush and ice in shifting bands, making her strain for a sight line.

She slid up the ramp, found the road, and made the turn into town with just the slightest bucking and fishtailing, like riding an almost-broke horse.

"Holy shit," she said aloud to no one. "Holy shit. Jesus."

She took it easy through Hot Springs, found the street Eve had listed as her next turn, and without a choice—since, as much as she would have liked to stop and wait until the storm had blown over and things had settled down, she didn't know a soul in any of these little houses with their lights on and smoke coming out of their chimneys—she headed once again out of town. She had to get to Mule Creek Junction, where there was nothing and no one even on the sunniest day, and make a left.

If the snow got too deep she could always turn back, she told herself, leaving the town behind her, praying that the deserted grasslands ahead might be clear, that the rural plows might have already come through so that the way marked out in Eve's directions would be open.

Finally arriving at the Babbitts'—nearly ten hours after pulling out of her own driveway—René hauled her suitcase up the crumbling steps. Inside, birds screamed, cats ran, and Kat and Mrs. Babbitt came scampering to greet her. They had news, they said.

"*Saaaad* news," Mrs. Babbitt sang, hanging her head.

They'd had to move Mrs. Babbitt's father into a nursing home. His pain had gotten too bad. It was overwhelming, for everyone. The worst part was that he hadn't wanted to go, they said. Enraged and helpless, he'd screamed at Mrs. Babbitt, calling her names.

"Even slapped her," Kat whispered.

Mrs. Babbitt started to cry. "I would have kept him here forever. I wanted to. I tried to."

Kat put her arm around her mother's shoulder, moving her to the couch.

"We've been so blessed in this house." Mrs. Babbitt looked wistfully around the room as tears rolled fat and heavy down her cheeks. "But with Papa gone, and with what that's going to cost— Well— We're going to have to move, maybe find a little apartment." She dabbed at her eyes with a dingy hankie. "I'm sorry, René. I know you were counting on us. We can wait for you to find a place. No hurry. Please don't worry."

"Don't cry, Mommy," Kat said.

"It's all right, Kittykat. Everything in its own time. I'll be better."

Mrs. Babbitt lifted her glasses from where they'd settled on the tip of her nose and wiped her eyes. Then she put them back on, pushing them up, and sniffled, making a quiet, involuntary gasp as she straightened her scarf. She blew her nose and the birds squawked.

Kat leaned her head onto her mother's shoulder.

"I'm sorry about your dad," René said, marveling at the tenderness in front of her, astounded by the genuine feeling this mother and daughter seemed to share, their complete lack of animosity, their mutual innocence, as though they were missing an essential component, something the rest of the world relied on to stay upright.

Still—buzzing from the harrowing drive, and now finding herself displaced—she was having trouble following the emotional arc of what was unfolding at the Babbitts'. To her, it seemed that the old man ending up in a nursing home was a given, that he likely should have been sent off a long time ago.

"It's okay," she added. "I can try to find something."

"Thank you, dear," Mrs. Babbitt said. "I don't want you to feel rushed. We'll all work together and make sure it works out. For *eeeeverybody*. Okay?"

René nodded and took her suitcase to the room across the hall from where the old man used to be. When school started in the morning, first she'd look for Dan, to tell him how much Al had liked his drawing. "He loved it," she repeated, practicing, reminding herself that it didn't matter whether it was true or not. "He loved it so much he's going to frame it and hang it up!" Then she'd look for Janet and tell her about the Babbitts, to see if she might have a good idea about what to do next.

42

WHEN THEY FIRST PASSED IN THE HALL, DAN raised his eyebrows and winked at her. René wanted to go up to him right then to say what she'd been planning to say, but he had his arm around an older girl, a senior, and the girl was not only holding on to the hand Dan had flung over her shoulder but also grabbing him around the waist, talking and laughing, her voice ringing through the hallway. René bobbed her head in a quick hello and kept going, feeling the girl glare as they passed.

So Dan had a girlfriend. Which must have happened over Christmas. And which explained why he hadn't called. Somehow the worst of it was that the girl wasn't even pretty. Her yellow hair was slick and stringy, her skin pockmarked, her teeth already gone dark from smoking. René could picture her sitting at a kitchen table piled high with dirty dishes, lighting up a smoke, reaching into an open box of Fruit Loops as the TV blared. So how was she with Dan? It didn't make sense.

Still, Dan smiled whenever they passed, catching her eye as though there was something he wanted to say to her—as though, more than anything, he wanted to be free of that girl so he could come over and talk.

"Forget it," Janet told her. "Just forget about him. He's in a fog. Might as well be a zombie."

It was Janet's theory that the yellow-haired girl was giving Dan everything he'd ever wanted.

"He's not going to leave her. Not now. Not with all the head he's been getting in the parking lot. No way."

Which was shocking, unimaginable.

Dan never called her again, so she never got to deliver the lines she'd rehearsed about his drawing and how much Al had liked it. And he never stopped to give her a ride to school.

She still saw him speeding past her each day at the bus stop, now with three up in the cab of his pickup—the homely yellow-haired girl in the middle. But whenever he tried to wave, like he used to, the girl would smack his arm down, and when his truck backfired—on purpose or by accident, René never knew—the three of them would rock in their seats, laughing and slapping their legs.

43

A FEW DAYS AFTER RENÉ TOLD JANET ABOUT needing to move out of the Babbitts', Janet started talking about René coming to live with *her*—saying she wouldn't have to charge much for room and board since René could babysit from time to time, so René's parents would save money and Janet could maybe even go out on a date or something.

"Talk about your wildest dream," Janet said, rolling her eyes. They could live together and help each other. That was the gist. They could talk and hang out. "Not like a teacher," Janet said. "Like friends. Like a big sister or something."

Which made René smile, thinking of hanging out with Janet every day. Janet—who knew so many things, who was always ready with advice and guidance, who'd be there for you no matter what.

The next weekend they took a trip up to the Rockies with Janet's little daughter, Gigi, and spent the day laughing and having snowball fights, pulling Gigi behind them in her sled. It was the most fun René could remember having, maybe ever. As the sun began to sink—the snow forming a dazzling blue crust under the shimmering pines—they went out for hot chocolates, then drove to Boulder, to Janet's mother's house, where there was a fire in the fireplace, a pot roast in the oven, and where everyone welcomed René like long-lost family.

René and Janet set up a room in Janet's basement—putting down an area rug to cover the concrete floor, hanging a curtain to hide the exposed water heater, hauling in a twin bed from Janet's brother's storage unit. And each day, after René got home from school and dance class, they'd put Gigi to bed, then sit in the kitchen and talk—René eating graham crackers, Janet pouring herself a tumbler of wine from a box in the refrigerator. For René, it was like stepping out of a dark room and into the sunshine. She basked in the light of Janet's gaze, as Janet tossed her feathery blond hair and told stories, laughing about all the people she knew who were getting divorced because of torrid love affairs, and the people who were sleeping with people they shouldn't be sleeping with, trying and failing to not get caught.

"You can't always follow the rules," Janet would say. "God knows, you can't be acting uptight all the time. Not if you ever want to get what you want out of life."

Mostly, it seemed, Janet talked about sex and school, especially who at school was having sex—who was having a little and who was having a lot, who maybe hadn't done it yet but was getting close. According to Janet, nearly everyone at school, teachers included, was having sex all the time—in the front seats of cars, under the bleachers in the gym, in doorways between classes, girls leaning back into corners, hitching up their skirts. Which wasn't so hard to believe, seeing Dan and the yellow-haired girl in the hallways each day—his hand resting on her shoulder, hers stuffed into the back pocket of his jeans.

And, finally opening her eyes to the signs—couples sheepishly darting through the halls, teachers giving each other secret smiles—René started to see that Janet was right, that everybody but her seemed to have a boyfriend, that everyone but her was, like Janet said, "most likely *doing it*."

44

"What you need is an older guy. Somebody who knows his way around," Janet said one day. "I've had plenty of guys. And not just my ex. There've been lots of guys. God knows. What *you* need is a good start. That's what."

The only older guy René could think of was Marcus.

Marcus had recently joined their ballet class. He wasn't a dancer, exactly, but he'd been a bodybuilder and a gymnast, so he was clearly an athlete. Dicker kept telling him that if only he worked hard enough all his training would transfer and he'd pick up ballet easily. Which definitely wasn't happening. Marcus tromped across the floor like a linebacker, his feet shuffling mysteriously through improvised steps—vaguely similar to what the rest of the class was doing, but different. Still, he had the body for it—like a statue—though a little wide across the shoulders due to his weight lifting.

"There's your detriment, Marcus!" Dicker would call across the room, correcting him again and again, loud and teasing. "There's your downfall, Marcus! There's your Achilles' heel, Marcus!"

"What's he talking about?" Marcus would joke after class. "Does anybody know?"

Marcus had sandy-blond hair like a surfer kid and light blue eyes like tropical water reflecting the clearest sky, and he was constantly in a good mood, always prepared with something sweet and senseless to make you laugh.

One day after class Marcus asked René if she could make him a pair of tie-front pants, like the ones she'd made for herself in sewing class. So she sat on the floor in front of him and measured his inseam, running her tape up the insides of his legs as he giggled, promising over and over to stop being so ticklish.

"I'm trying. Just stop," he laughed, jumping away. "Gimme a break." He turned around, took few deep breaths, then turned back, beaming idiotically.

She measured around his waist, around his hips with him holding the tape measure in front, then down the outside of his legs. And he insisted on paying her.

"I don't care what you say," he said after she told him not to worry about it, that she was happy to make him the pants. "Here." He handed her some folded cash. "These pants are gonna be so goddamn cool. Everybody's gonna want 'em. You just wait."

She made him the pants and they fit perfectly.

"I'm gonna wear these every day," he said, modeling his new pants, turning side to side. He did a silly tour jeté by the front reception desk of the dance studio. "All—day—long!"

"No, you are not, Marcus," Dicker put in, passing between the two of them in his three-piece suit and shiny loafers. "You most certainly will not. I forbid it." He smiled coyly at Marcus, then, because she was standing there, offered a similar look in René's direction, lingering to survey her up and down.

"You might want to start thinking about your weight, dear," he said offhandedly. "If you still want to go to New York, that is. Just a word of caution."

If she still wanted to go to New York? What was he talking about? Of course she still wanted to go to New York. What else was she doing here but trying to get out of high school so she could go to New York?

He looked back to Marcus. "And you in those pants!" He raised his eyebrows and grinned. "Nothing short of an insult to eyesight."

After Dicker had gone into the men's changing room, Marcus rolled his eyes and said, "He's kind of an asshole, but he knows a lot about ballet, right?"

René figured she agreed with him on the first point but was unsure about the second.

"I love these, René," he went on, unfazed. "They're so awesome. I don't give a shit what that old fart says. I'm gonna wear 'em all the time." He laughed.

To thank her for the "awesome pants," Marcus wanted to take her to lunch.

"I guess I could get away," she said, her face going hot. Was she blushing? "I've got study break at eleven."

"Perfect," Marcus said, putting his hand on her shoulder. "I know just the place. One of those hidden gems."

45

She stepped into the old Victorian to find Marcus waiting in the foyer. He took her coat and, gallantly standing at attention, offered his arm like a regimental soldier.

"Second floor," he said, leading her up the wide staircase.

The house was empty and quiet, and for a moment René let herself imagine that Marcus was leading her up to his bedroom. Which would have been fine by her. After all the talking with Janet, she was more than ready to be ushered into that secret place Janet couldn't seem to stop waxing on about—that magical garden continuously blooming in oversaturated colors.

A waitress led them past a dozen empty tables set with linens and small flowers.

"A little early for the regular crowd," Marcus whispered, resting a hand on her hip.

And once they were seated in the corner by the window, she followed his lead—unfolding her napkin, placing it across her lap—as Marcus leaned in.

"You'd never know this place existed if you didn't already know about it, right?"

Though she'd passed the old house a thousand times on her way to school, she would have never guessed it was a restaurant.

"How'd you find it?" she asked. Because as far as she knew, Marcus had been in Denver for even less time than she had.

"Oh," Marcus said, the color rising in his cheeks. "A friend brought me. I love it. And I love those pants you made me. So I wanted to bring you."

And the waitress was back with their menus.

After lunch, Marcus said he wanted to take her out sometime, to an after-hours club he knew about. When she reminded him that she wasn't nearly old enough for anything like that, he told her that he knew the people who ran the place, that he'd talk to them, that it'd be fine.

"It doesn't open till late," he warned. "I don't know if you can get away."

And anticipating the look on Janet's face when she told her that not only had Marcus asked her out on a date, but that he'd asked her to stay out *late*—and they both knew what *that* meant—René assured him she'd be there.

"I have a car. I can drive," she said, thinking how she'd already been breaking all the promises she made to Eve—not to drive her grandma's car to school or to ballet, not to drive it around town, like not having a car at all. Eve! With all her restrictions and resentments and not a romantic bone in her body. "I'll meet you," she said.

"Great. Now if only *I* can get away." Marcus laughed.

And though René had no idea what he was talking about, she smiled, laughing along. She was game for whatever Marcus had in mind. She wanted to be sure he knew that.

Marcus reached under the table, taking hold of her hands. "I like you, René," he whispered. "I think you're the coolest."

"I like you, too, Marcus."

And with a tidal wave silently swelling inside her, she looked into Marcus's sea-blue eyes and nodded until there was no room for doubt.

46

Dicker started talking about a spring recital, about some old ballet friend of his coming to do a staging of *Le Sacre du Printemps*—"The Sacrificial Orgy," he called it, smiling and looking over at Marcus, who quickly lowered his eyes and shuffled his feet like he was marking out a country-western line dance.

The show would be *Sacre* plus something original, Dicker said. "Not everyone will have a part. Prepare yourselves. I don't want any bellyaching." Then he turned and walked out of the studio calling, "Marcus, come. Don't dillydally!"

Marcus rolled his eyes at René, loitering—bending to touch his toes, looking in the mirror, stretching side to side.

He and René had plans to meet at the late-night club on Wednesday.

"Not the weekend?" she'd asked when he first mentioned Wednesday, thinking she'd likely gotten her signals crossed.

"To be discreet," Marcus said, smiling like they shared a secret. "So we can have privacy."

Which was just what she'd been hoping.

Now he came up behind her, putting his hand on her

shoulder. "I have to change to Thursday," he whispered. "Does Thursday work?"

She nodded.

"Sorry," Marcus said. "I—" He stopped. "Thursday, then."

He let his hand rest on the back of her neck for a split second, then moved on, headed for the dressing room. Dicker would be waiting for him, likely to give him further corrections on technique and notes on the mistakes he'd made in class, and Marcus was clearly less than enthusiastic. As he reached for the doorknob he glanced back at René, shaking his head. "Sacrificial orgy," he whispered sarcastically. "What a weirdo."

47

Though René had imagined a club with flashing lights and a glittering dance floor, the place Marcus took her was, once again, in a quiet downtown Victorian. At the top of the stairs this time she found a single L-shaped room lined with deep red velvet banquettes, where couples sat smoking, talking, drinking. There was a long mahogany bar and, behind it, reflected in the gold-etched mirrors, every conceivable shape and shade of liquor bottle.

As she and Marcus edged into one of the booths, a man in a perfectly fitted dark suit, his collar turned crisply over a broad silk tie, approached, extending his hand.

"Marcus. Pleasure." He shook Marcus's hand, then tilted his head, suggesting Marcus follow. So Marcus got up.

The man stood about a foot taller than Marcus. He bent as Marcus gestured, nodding and looking over at René, which made her understand that they were going over the problem of her age. And since she tended to look more like twelve than sixteen—much less eighteen—she turned away, waiting quietly.

"No problem," Marcus said when he got back. "But I had to

promise we'd be no trouble. No trouble," he repeated, pointing at her. "That means *you*." He smiled and René laughed, relieved.

"You want a drink? How about a brandy Alexander? You like that?"

"I could try it."

"You'll like it. You will."

Marcus went up to the bar and came back with what looked like two frothy milkshakes in tall parfait glasses.

"Doubles," he said, grinning. "So we don't have to get up."

They toasted and drank, and René instantly felt a warmth spreading from her throat and chest to every extremity.

"So," Marcus said.

"So," René echoed.

"Here we are. We got away."

René smiled, thinking how nothing could have been more apt and insightful.

"Tell me about yourself," Marcus said. "I wanna know everything."

And though she started with leaving home, René didn't even get to the part about getting kicked out of the Sheads' and having to leave Phoenix and move to Denver before they were sitting close—his arm around her, her head on his shoulder, his lips so close, closer—him suddenly kissing her so deeply, mixing the heat and sweetness of their drinks until they were sharing one taste, one breath, making any need for talking simply vanish, every dull formality obliterated.

They made out for what seemed like hours, the room dissolving around them, the heady buzz of the club covering them like a blanket so that right there in public they were hidden and alone. They paused in unison to take a sip of their drinks before leaning in again, unable to help themselves, both wanting only one thing, the same thing—whatever was *here, now, this.*

They ended up so far down in their banquette that the man in the suit came over and tapped Marcus on the shoulder. "No lying down, brother," he said. So they straightened up, arranging themselves, and the man nodded, then went to turn down the lights.

Their first double brandies were finished, so Marcus said he'd get a second round but first he had to sit awhile.

"Talk to me," he said, his cheeks flushed, his eyes shining as he lifted her hand, kissing it. "I think you're gonna have to talk to me for a minute before I can stand up. Where were you in that story anyway? I got lost."

And for no discernable reason—except perhaps the inanity of any story or explanation either of them might have to offer at a time like this—they started to laugh. They laughed so hard they nearly fell down in their booth all over again.

René leaned into him. A languid Spanish song was playing over the general club noise. "You should go dance on that bar," she said. "I'll watch you."

"What? I can't even stand up right now," Marcus laughed. "And not because I'm too drunk, either. I don't think I'm even drunk at all." He kissed her.

"Go on, then. Why not?"

"I can't." He continued to kiss her. "Because of you," he said. "You. *You*. And don't kiss me now. Stop. Please. I'm about to have a big problem. God."

So they sat together and Marcus pointed out people he said he'd seen before. The old guy with the purple bow tie was here every night, so drunk he could barely walk. Marcus had never seen him not plastered. And the lady in the lime-green dress had more money than God. That's what people said.

"Do you come here a lot?" René asked.

"Sometimes." Marcus looked away.

He finally shook himself and stood, smoothing his clothes, paying special attention to pulling the front of his trousers straight, giving René a goofy surfer-boy grin.

When he came back with their drinks they clinked glasses. The lights now lower, the place clearing out—they started in where they'd left off. And after another long spell of coming up only for brief intervals of drinking and air, Marcus began to whisper about where they might go.

"I don't really have a place," he said, mumbling something about a roommate. "Can we go to your place?"

Her place? She was in high school. She didn't have a *place*. It was one thing to talk on and on with Janet about having sex, another to bring a man into the house to actually do it. Plus she'd only been at Janet's for a few months. She had to be careful.

So they stayed at the club, the man at the door looking away as they fell into each other, going as far as they could—resting and pulling ahead and resting and pulling ahead, like long-distance swimmers.

Outside in the dark Marcus leaned René up against her grandma's car.

"We'll find a way," he said, tucking her hair behind her ear, gently stroking her cheek. "I can hardly stand this. I'm gonna work on it."

He was pressing into her, holding her head in his hands, kissing her so deeply that the idea of two bodies standing there was relative.

"I have to stop, I have to stop," he breathed, kissing her again and again. Then he stopped, stepping back awkwardly, standing under the streetlight. "See you at class," he said.

"See you at class."

He opened her car door and she got in, rolling her window down, taking his hand. Then she pulled away from where he stood, reluctantly, waving as he waved.

48

Marcus did the same adorable hopping about as usual in class—smiling and shuffling his feet, shaking his sandy-blond hair at the end of each combination as if he'd just stepped out of a wave. He'd accidentally-on-purpose bump shoulders with René as they passed on their way to the changing rooms, but other than that, he never gave the slightest indication that they were anything but ballet friends. So she kept it to herself, too, grinning but keeping her distance.

After class one night, Dicker made an announcement. His choreographer friend would be arriving in the next few weeks, so he needed to start assigning roles. He'd be speaking to everyone individually.

René shot Marcus an excited look, and he raised his crossed fingers at her, jumping foot to foot like a boxer until Dicker caught his eye in the mirror and held it, and Marcus, admonished, turned to face the barre, stretching out his calves and peering down at the floor. Though René glanced back at him, he didn't raise his head or look her way. Then Dicker marched out of the studio calling, "Marcus, come!" So Marcus picked up his bag and turned to follow.

As Marcus passed, he reached to graze René's hip. She turned to him, mouthing *Sorry,* thinking maybe she'd gotten him in trouble for goofing off while Dicker was talking, but he shook his head and mouthed back *No,* like it was nothing at all, just the usual bullshit from Dicker.

49

Some already knew what they'd be dancing, letting it float through the class, whispered from one to the next. Dicker's favorite, the older girl, Marcie—who'd given up on New York and now worked in a real estate office downtown—would be the lead in the original choreography.

"Marcie's been Mr. D's prima for years," Mrs. Babbitt said in the dressing room, giving the word a weight it couldn't possibly carry, as if just saying it made it mean something.

Kat—whose birdlike body chopped up the air, her legs and arms carving awkward right angles—was in *Sacre,* in the corps. Mrs. Babbitt was so excited she looked to be hooked up to an electrical wire.

But René was still waiting to hear, telling herself that it was likely good to have this prolonged delay, that it probably meant she was being considered for something special, something that required thought and deliberation.

And all the while Dicker's color was high—his cheeks the shade of raw hamburger.

Then one night after nearly everyone else had left the studio, Dicker invited René into his "office," as he called it, opening the door to the men's changing room.

"Don't worry, dear," he said when she hung back. "They've all gone home. Just you and me." And he smiled at her like she was a small child.

Was he finally going to give her a part? Would she be the sacrificial princess? Or maybe there was a new role, a solo, just for her?

Dicker led her through an interior door in the men's changing area, into a small separate room—like a closet—with a desk, a chair, a tall filing cabinet. There was barely enough space for the two of them.

It was all disorienting: her being in the men's room, Dicker's having an office. She thought he'd been making a joke. Dicker was a ballet teacher who dressed like a dandy, calling out combinations half-heartedly, his attention wandering until he found himself in the mirror. So, he had an office? *But—what for?*

He closed the door behind her, shutting them in, then flexed his hip and rested his elbow high on the metal cabinet.

"I hear you and Marcus have become friendly," he started, raising his head at her, seeming to challenge her in a way she couldn't make out.

"A little," she tried, confused.

"You *do* understand why you're here, correct?"

Dicker paused, so she nodded.

"You're on scholarship," he said, his nostrils flaring.

"Which your mother insisted on, I might remind you—and which comes directly out of *my* pocket."

Startled by the sudden, palpable hostility, René took a step back and found herself up against the door.

Dicker stopped—dropping his arm, tugging on his vest to straighten it, obviously trying to quell some kind of fury.

"I thought you were serious about your dancing," he went on, giving her a haughty, contemptuous look. "But it seems I was wrong,"

"You're not wrong," she said, feeling herself go pale. She'd been in class every night all year. She'd come to class even when she'd had to miss school because of a fever and croupy cough—bronchitis, it turned out—and even though Dicker routinely ignored her, walking past her without so much as turning his head.

"Don't pretend you don't know what I'm talking about!" Dicker cried, his voice suddenly shrill, piercing. "You're supposed to be studying, not wasting your time with Marcus! He's no good for you! You stay away from him!"

"But—"

For a split second René wondered if she shouldn't be honest with Dicker, if she shouldn't make an effort to trust him. Maybe she could tell him how Marcus made her feel—how when she was with him she felt cool and smart and funny.

Dicker stepped away from the filing cabinet, moving toward her with the cast of a man on his deathbed—his translucent skin ashen, his delicate hands trembling. There was obviously more at stake here than she knew—something she hadn't seen, something she'd missed.

"*You!*" Dicker extended his index finger at her like a jackknife, pointing it into her face.

There was nowhere to go.

"*You*! You stay away from Marcus! You hear me? Marcus is *mine*! You stay away from him. I'm telling you now, and I won't tell you again. Do you understand? I'm warning you. You have no business with Marcus. No business and no right!"

René began to bob her head, nodding repeatedly.

"Do you understand me? It's very important. Imperative!"

She kept nodding.

"Say it!" Dicker screamed at her.

"I understand," René said.

"All right, then."

Dicker lowered his hand and began to preen—stepping back and smoothing his suit jacket, pulling out and refolding his pocket square as if to calm himself.

"As long as you do," he said, still visibly shaking.

And after a moment of charged silence, he turned away. "That's all. You can go," he said. "But I expect you to remember what we've talked about. Marcus is not for you." He turned back. "Marcus is taken."

And, grappling for the doorknob behind her, René let herself out through the men's room, stumbling down the steps and into the street.

50

WITH ONLY THE STREETLIGHT TO GUIDE HER, she opened the car door and felt her legs go wobbly. She fell into her grandma's car, breathing unsteadily, her body cold and trembling, as if she'd been packed in ice. *Heartbreak, sadness, ruin:* the sudden chasm between where she'd thought she was and where she found herself to be.

No role for her. No role at all.

And no Marcus. Marcus was a phantom.

She'd been fooled, accosted, robbed.

All that remained was Dicker screaming—*You! You stay away from him! Stay away!*

And she was left—empty-handed and powerless—to face the facts. She'd have to get up in the morning and go to school. She'd have to be in ballet class every day without betraying her distress. If she let go the least hateful word, or gave Dicker the slightest vengeful look, it would all be over. She'd be asked to leave. And how would she explain it all to Eve? And where would she go this time?

She cried all night in Janet's basement, wondering what

she'd done wrong. Still, she came upstairs the next morning and the morning after that and faced Janet's questions, trying to explain how stupid she'd been, how she hadn't understood, hadn't looked closely enough, hadn't seen what was right in front of her, how she'd been blind, wanting only what she wanted, wanting Marcus.

She went to school and to ballet, every day, steeling herself with the thought that, in the end, Dicker wasn't going to win. Because, unlike the rest of Dicker's students, René wasn't staying in Denver. She was going to New York. And Dicker had nothing to do with that. Neither Dicker nor Marcus had anything to do with that at all. It was *hers,* the one thing that actually belonged to her, the only thing that really mattered.

So regardless of what might happen from here on—Dicker could keep ignoring her in class and refuse to give her the slightest role; Marcus could pretend there was nothing at all between them—she was going to be in class doing adagio, allegro, pirouette, grand jeté, waltz step across the floor. She was going to be there every day, getting ready to put this useless Denver pit stop behind her.

51

It wasn't a week later that Dicker came into the studio with his head wrapped in a bandage and his neck in a brace, Marcus right behind him, carrying his bags, looking chagrined.

"Nothing, nothing," Dicker said, waving people away as they gasped at his swollen purple cheek. "A minor accident. Nothing to be concerned about." But his speech was lopsided, as if he'd just come from the dentist's.

In the dressing room after class, Mrs. Babbitt whispered quietly to René that she'd heard it was Marcus who'd done that to Dicker, that they'd been arguing, that Marcus had slammed Dicker's head into their headboard.

That's how she said it—*their* headboard. *Theirs.* Like it was an established fact, like everyone else had known all along.

"I'm telling you because I'm concerned," Mrs. Babbitt went on. "Mr. Dicker could have been killed! I've been watching."

Mrs. Babbitt confided that she'd been worried since the moment Marcus first showed up—out of the blue with no place to live.

"Out of nothing less than the kindness of his heart Mr. Dicker took him in. And now look." She shook her head. "I don't want to say it, but it can be a burden to be too kindhearted. And to end up like this?"

It was mind-boggling the way Mrs. Babbitt was so obviously in love with Dicker—which was likely what kept her coming to class each night. Still, René felt a click, like she could finally see straight.

Marcus was young and beautiful—charming, sensual, enthusiastic—and he'd needed somewhere to stay. Enter Dicker, who'd spent a lifetime looking for just such a young man. They'd hit it off, Marcus had moved in, and—for the price of a place to call home, for the comfort of belonging somewhere in the world—Marcus was Dicker's prisoner.

She could see it all now—something as light and mundane as Marcus saying to her that night at the club, as they melted into each other in their soft velvet booth, "We got away," suddenly stocked with meaning, and "I don't really have a place," now clear as crystal. And here it was, laid out in front of her—Dicker in a bandage and neck brace, Marcus looking away.

Day after day Dicker continued to walk the studio, calling out the combinations feebly, not turning his head. Still, he went after Marcus with renewed vigor, both in and out of class: "Marcus, put down that apple! Marcus, stop eating those grapes! Why do you constantly have to be putting something in your mouth? Look at yourself!" Then he'd tilt his head gently, restrained by his neck brace, and give Marcus an impish grin as Marcus stood stock-still, his pale cheeks on fire.

Marcus never approached René about what had happened between the two of them—or with her and Dicker, or with Dicker and him, none of it. And though she liked to imagine that Marcus had pummeled Dicker because of her—because of how Dicker had threatened her, since the timing was right—she knew it could just as easily have been some botched version of whatever it was they were doing together.

Whatever had happened, Marcus was staying away from her just like she was staying away from him.

And one day, when she'd finally given up expecting it, René got her assigned role for the spring recital, communicated through Marcie—the "prima," the girl who'd chosen to play the local dance studio queen instead of dancing with a real ballet company.

René was going to be in *Sacre*. Just like Kat. One ballet, landlocked in the corps, where the goal was to be invisible.

52

"Jim Davis is driving to South Dakota to visit some cousins," Janet said one day, unpacking groceries onto the counter. "He says he's fine with giving you a ride if you want to go for Easter."

René's teacher, Mr. Davis, had thick brown hair and a tall, muscular build. Back in the fall, when she'd been in his class, he'd talked mainly about his pickup basketball games and his softball team, and whenever he'd stood by her desk, she'd felt a swift diffusion of her blood that had made her go woozy, like her bones were melting.

She'd taken his Family Planning class along with his History of Cinema, where he'd pulled down the shades, turned out the lights, and they'd watched one movie after the next in the darkened room. She'd had to restrain herself from turning around to take yet another look at him there, sitting on the window ledge—arms crossed, legs spread—leaning back into the blackout shades.

She was waiting on Janet's front steps, her overnight bag at her feet, when Mr. Davis pulled up to the curb and got out of his car, opening the back door.

"Hi, Mr. Davis!" she called, running down the walk. "You want me to ride in the back?"

He laughed, taking her bag and tossing it in.

"I'm happy to drive you, but I'm not gonna be your chauffeur. And you can't call me Mr. Davis all the way to South Dakota. Better get that straight. Get in front. And call me Jim. You're not in my class anymore."

She got in, giddy to be sitting in the same car with *Jim,* feeling like she was riding with the wind in her hair even though all the windows were rolled up. It was still cold in Denver—light whiffs of spring carried on the breeze, but nothing you could count on.

Just a few miles out of town, her seat belt alarm started sounding. She unbuckled and buckled back up, but it didn't stop. It only stopped when she lifted herself out of her seat.

"That happens sometimes," Jim Davis said.

"I could get in back."

"There's not much room back there."

She turned to find his duffel and her bag on top of boxes piled up to the windows.

"I'm taking books and stuff to my cousin in Black Hawk," he said over the beeping. "She teaches school out there, so I collect things for her."

"That's nice."

René lifted herself out of her seat to stop the maddening

noise. When she sat back down the alarm started screaming all over again.

"Just scoot over," Jim said. "Sit in the middle."

She hesitated. But Jim Davis wasn't some creep like Mrs. Beech's grandson. Jim Davis was her teacher. Jim Davis was Jim Davis. And the seat belt alarm was making her reluctance look ridiculous.

So she budged over.

Jim found a baseball game on the radio and explained the plays as the sportscaster called them. He drove a different route from the one she was used to, so it was all new to her until they reached Custer. By then, he was resting his large forearm on her leg.

"Wanna take a back road?" he said.

"Does it go to Rapid?"

"I think so. Who knows?" He laughed and she laughed with him, thinking he must be teasing.

So he turned off the highway onto a deserted gravel road, and once they were under the cover of towering pines, he pulled over and cut the engine.

"You wanna sit on my lap?" he asked, resting his arm along the seatback behind her.

Did she want to sit on his lap? She'd wanted to sit on his lap since the beginning of the school year when he'd first stood in front of their Family Planning class and asked who was going to stay a virgin until they were married. How naïve she'd been back then!

"Do you want me to?"

He nodded.

She could feel her face going red. Because Jim Davis wasn't just a high school kid, like Dan, and in no way was he like Marcus. He was older, and he was serious.

"Come on, then," he said. "Get on over here."

He held her leg to help her straddle him, and she took hold of his broad shoulders to steady herself, ending up with the steering wheel behind her. He settled his hands on her back—untucking her blouse, pulling her toward him. They kissed. They kissed and he leaned back, pulling her along, running his large hands up to her neck and down to her waist, smoothing his hands over her thighs and down her legs as she marveled at her luck: *Jim Davis?*

He pushed her back to look at her.

"You're a surprise. I mean, I didn't expect it. God, you're like a doll. You're so pretty." He touched the side of her cheek, fanning her long hair out over her shoulder. Then, glancing off at something down the gravel road, he gave a start.

She turned to see a single police car cruising slowly toward them.

"Jesus," Jim Davis said, quickly lifting her off his lap and setting her back in her own seat, far over on the passenger side.

The cop passed without stopping. He even raised a hand to give Jim a wave.

"Shit," Jim said, starting the car. "All the way out here, in the middle of nowhere? Some cop? Jesus. That was close."

"But we weren't doing anything."

"Really?" Jim said, like she'd given the wrong answer in class. "Are you underage? Am I your teacher?"

"What's the big deal?" she said. "What does he care? I can do what I want."

"You can?" Jim finally smiled, loosening up, shaking it off, the cop now well out of sight. "Well, maybe you can, but you can't right here. Not now."

Then he got the car turned around and headed back to the highway and Rapid City.

"I'll call you," he said when he dropped her off. "It's weird. I wasn't really sure I wanted to make this trip, but now I can't wait to get back in the car." His sad smile accentuated his firm jaw and deep brown eyes.

She knew what he meant.

The ham, the colored eggs, the Easter candy was all a blur.

Eve hid plastic grass nests around the house for Jayne, and everyone was pretty cheerful—René peeling potatoes, Jayne making a salad, Al watching TV. Still, René was counting the hours, waiting for Jim Davis to call and tell her he was ready to go.

He called Sunday evening.

"I can't talk. I'll be there early, okay?"

So she spent the night watching holiday specials with Al and Jayne—barely registering the Jews lost in the desert and the Red Sea parting, then Christ dying on the cross and the stone rolling away—as Eve did the dishes and cleaned up the kitchen, leaving leftovers on the counter until it was time for bed.

In the morning she waved goodbye to her family and got back in the car with Jim.

The seat belt alarm didn't sound.

"You got it fixed," she said, after they'd pulled out of her driveway and turned onto Mount Rushmore Road, on their way out of town.

"Looks like it fixed itself," he said. "Too bad." He laughed. "God. That was the longest weekend." And once they were back in the hills, he patted the seat next to him and said, "Just get on over here." So she moved over, feeling her leg rest against his muscular thigh.

They had four hundred miles to go—four hundred miles to touch, lean, kiss. They listened to music and talked about what they were going to do when they got back. Jim was going to take her to his house, then call his teammates and tell them he couldn't make the game that night, they'd have to find another second baseman.

"Feels like I'm coming down with something," he groaned weakly, practicing.

She laughed.

"More than honest," he said, bending feverishly to kiss her neck as he drove.

53

SHE STOOD IN HIS BEDROOM, SHEEPISHLY TRYING to cover herself with her hands as he slowly stripped off her clothes. He unbuttoned his shirt, dropping it to the floor, then laid her gently back onto his bed, running his strong hands over her smooth body, spreading her legs, kissing her up and down, pushing himself against her, the creamy corduroy of his pants like velvet on her pale skin.

"I've never done this before," she said, breathing into his ear.

"What?" He was lost.

So she repeated it.

He stopped. "What? Wait. What? I didn't—" He lifted himself up, pulling away, shaking his head as if to wake himself.

"It's okay, Jim. Really." She was holding on to his thick upper arms, trying to pull him back to her. "I'm ready. I am. It's no big deal. Janet and I talk about it all the time, and it's going to happen someday, right? Come on. Come on, Jim. Please. We both want to."

With every word, every flailing plea, she could see she was talking him out of it.

"I didn't know," Jim said, helpless, turning to sit at the edge of his bed, his back to her now, head in his hands. "Jesus. It's not right. And Janet? Shit. Janet? Jesus, René. *Janet?*"

He stood, picking up his shirt from the floor, and left the room. So she got up, too, and put her clothes back on, gathering them from where he'd dropped them.

She found him on the sofa in the living room, dazed, as though he'd fallen there, his crumpled shirt buttoned only halfway. He was leaning back into the cushions, like she'd seen him so many times before, leaning into the dark window shades for movie class. She sat on the floor in front of him, her head in his lap.

"You have to go," he said, eyeing her tenderly but keeping his hands inert, heavy at his sides. "Really. You shouldn't be here. We can't do this."

René sat up, looking at him—disheveled and undone as he was, as they both were—not understanding. Was he rejecting her? Right in the middle of everything? Just because she was a virgin? Hadn't Janet said that what men wanted most was a girl who was innocent and pure?

"I'll call you," Jim said. "Promise. We'll talk. But you have to go. Now. Come on."

He took her by the shoulders and ushered her back out to the car. They got in and drove—this time not touching, not speaking, René staying over on her own side until Jim Davis dropped her off at Janet's.

In school, she watched for him between classes, but he always seemed to dodge her—passing quickly, deep in conversation with another teacher, purposely not looking her way. So she went to the office and told the secretary she needed to leave a note for Jim Davis.

The secretary looked confused.

"About a class last semester," René tried as she handed over the folded notepaper, where she'd written, *Call me. You said you'd call me. I can't wait anymore. I have to talk to you. You have to call.*

He called her. "You can't do that. They were wondering what you needed from me. I had to lie to them. You can't contact me, René. Really. We can't see each other. You're too young. You're gonna get me in trouble."

But hadn't he known how young she was when he first asked her to sit on his lap? Of course he had.

"But you—"

"I told you already. We can't do this, René. Really." He hung up.

So she waited, hoping his desire would override his good sense and he'd call to say something different—that he couldn't stop thinking about her, that he had to be with her, that he was dying for her.

When he didn't, she found Janet's faculty contact sheet and called him at home. He didn't answer, so she left a message.

The next day Janet came home fuming.

"Jim told me to tell you to stop calling him. You have to stop it, René. It's embarrassing. Plus, he could go to jail. Did you ever think of that? He could be in a shitload of trouble because of you." She was slamming around the kitchen like Eve sometimes did—putting things away, getting things out. "Whatever happened—it's over. He's sorry about it, but you have to stop bothering him. Just leave him alone. Jesus. He doesn't want to hear from you."

René had told Janet every detail of what had happened—how Jim Davis had taken off her clothes and lain on top of her, how he'd kissed every inch of her body, how René was now desperate to hear from him. But all Janet ever said was "Sounds like nothing, really. Just guys being guys."

René didn't call after that, and Jim didn't call. But the next thing René knew, Janet was telling her that Jim Davis was a mess, that he was dating a senior, a girl from school who'd had the same boyfriend since eighth grade. The poor boy was now spending his days wandering dejectedly through the hallways as the love of his life bounded along, glowing, pretending to be single even though everyone knew she was hot and heavy with Mr. Davis.

"Looks like she's on cloud nine for sure," Janet said. "And Jim. Good God. Talk about hog heaven."

Which made sense. Because not only did it seem like every other girl her age was ahead of her in every way that actually mattered—in figuring out about men, in knowing what to do with them and how to make them want you—but René had seen that girl, and that girl had it all. She was beautiful and sexy, and she hadn't been a virgin since she was maybe thirteen, was Janet's guess.

"She obviously knows her way around a man," Janet said one night as they sat at the kitchen table.

To which René could only nod, chastened, and sore at heart.

54

IN REHEARSALS EACH NIGHT THE PRIMA SQUABBLED with Dicker's other longtime students about how to count the music, while René kept quiet, buried in the circle of pagans gathered for the ritual sacrifice of the virgin.

Eve, Al, Jayne, and even Leon were driving down for the *Sacre* performance. René had sent them instructions on where to look for her onstage—drawing a map of the corps and circling her position. When she reminded Eve to bring binoculars, Eve just laughed.

"No, really," René said over the phone.

"I think I can recognize my own daughter."

"Not if you can't find me."

Then, after the performance—after they'd all congratulated her, telling her how much they'd liked it—Eve ended up confessing that, though they'd passed Al's field glasses back and forth, no one could say for sure that they'd actually seen her.

They were backstage with the other dancers and their families—Al looking like he was in an underground World

War II bunker, Leon facing into a far corner of the backstage hallway, frantically trying to light up a cigarette.

Leon had come back home to live, on hiatus from drinking and using, and he was agitated, constantly lingering in dark recesses, smoking and digging around in his pockets like he was looking for something he couldn't find.

"Get me outta here," he said when René went over to check on him.

She'd already introduced him around and everyone had been taken with him—his beautiful build, his dark wavy hair and kind eyes. She'd been telling people that she and Leon used to dance together back home as kids, that Leon was always a much better dancer than she was, that you could still see it in the way he walked.

"These guys all wanna shake my hand," he whispered, cocking his head, miming a limp-wristed handshake. "Just get me outta here, René. God. It's givin' me the creeps." He laughed.

He wasn't wrong.

Marcus—who'd danced the lead in every piece, jerking his body across the stage and jumping around on wooden feet—had disappeared with Dicker just after the performance, donning black tie and waving to the rest of them from above, like a movie star in a cologne ad. But the other men from René's class had been milling around Leon. He'd taken to the distant corner to avoid them.

Janet and her little daughter, Gigi, were staying at a friend's house so that René and her family would have the place to themselves. Leon took long walks, then spent the day on the couch—either asleep with the TV going or smoking one cigarette after the next down to the filter, not speaking—and Jayne played by herself in Gigi's room, sifting through the toys, or lay on the floor in the front room with Leon, staring at the television, while René sat with Eve and Al at the kitchen table, wondering what to talk about, wondering if they even knew one another anymore.

She clearly wasn't the same girl she'd been when she first left home. She'd been through lots of things she could never explain, things they could never imagine. So she was different now, which was something they didn't seem to want to know.

And one morning, after complaining over breakfast about all the time she'd wasted in Denver—about Dicker, his shabby students, the recital, her paltry role, about how she still needed to get to New York, how that was only going to be harder now—René ended up accidentally slipping into the arena of her ongoing talks with Janet. A distant alarm sounding at the back of her head, she heard herself telling Eve and Al that she'd be more than willing to live with a man without getting married. That she didn't see anything wrong with that. If only someone would want her.

And why not tell them? she thought. They were her parents, weren't they? They were the ones who were supposed to be helping her deal with things, helping her learn about life.

"I don't understand. *What* did you just say?" Eve said, instantly ignited, as Al went pale. "Do I need to wash your mouth out with soap, young lady? What is it, exactly, you've been learning down here? Just what have we been paying for?"

"Oh, don't pretend you were pure as snow on your wedding night," René countered, catching Eve's tone and flinging it right back, just like old times.

She remembered the girlhood photos of Eve with her friends—girls lined up out in the snow in bikinis, posing like pinups, pretending to take swigs from a bottle of ketchup. Eve was even younger than René when those photos were taken—her hair wild, a hand on her hip, one knee bent, her bare toes pointed into a snowbank. Eve and Al had been boyfriend-girlfriend since Eve was just fifteen. They'd gotten married on Eve's eighteenth birthday.

"Just *what* are you talking about?" Eve said, vicious.

Eve knew what René was talking about.

"I'm talking about a boyfriend! I'm talking about *sex*!"

Al's eyes widened. He exhaled, coughing, and got up to leave the room.

"Well?" René demanded.

"I can *not* believe what I'm hearing." Eve shook her head and started violently clearing away the dishes.

"I'm not a kid anymore, Mom."

"The hell you're not. Maybe you'd like to try supporting yourself for a while. Maybe that would help clear things up for you."

"Stop avoiding the question!" René shouted. "I'm not a baby!"

"Then stop acting like one!"

Eve turned to the sink and began angrily scrubbing the dishes as an unchecked tear escaped down René's cheek.

It was the last day of their visit. They'd be leaving in the morning.

"I'm not so sure this is working out," Eve said, her back still turned. "I have my doubts."

"No shit," René said. And as she got up to make a show of storming off to her bedroom in the basement, she could hear Al starting after Leon, telling him to get up, to get his feet off the couch.

"You can't just keep living like a goddamn freeloader in someone else's house, on someone else's dime! Wake up, Leon! For crying out loud, get up, why don't you! Do something useful!"

It was good they were going home. She was just glad she didn't have to go with them.

55

A FEW DAYS AFTER THE FAMILY LEFT, THERE WAS a knock on the door. Since René had been skipping Saturday classes—happy to miss the jam-up in Dicker's mixed-level weekend ordeal, where she had to battle fifth and sixth graders for enough space at the barre to do a simple battement or développé—she was on the floor playing Barbies with Gigi, passing the headless Ken back and forth, chatting about Barbie's clothes and how Barbie and Ken were in love and going to get married. She'd helped Gigi change Barbie into a wedding dress and tape Ken's head back onto his stump of a neck, getting them ready to walk down the aisle.

Janet answered the door.

"What in the hell?" she said before she even got it open. "All the way from Texas and you can't even call? What the hell, Ricky?"

"So now I gotta make an appointment?" Ricky said, stepping in. "A man's gotta see his baby girls, don't he?" He hugged Janet around the waist, hefting her into the air and turning her in a circle as Gigi looked up in surprise and alarm.

"Jesus!" Janet said. "Put me down!" So he plopped her down.

"Come see Papa," Ricky said, extending his arms to where Gigi and René were playing. But Gigi stayed where she was, bracing her hand against René's knee.

"What's this?" Ricky said. "You know your papa."

Janet came over, picked up Gigi, and carried her to the man suddenly standing in their living room. "You can't expect that, Ricky," she said. "You're not around. Remember? You have to at least give her a chance."

Ricky put his arms around both of them. "Family," he said, closing his eyes like he was drunk.

"Family, my ass," Janet said. "Let go of me. Really, Ricky. What the hell are you doing here?"

"A little visit with my family," he said, slapping her behind. "There's a problem with that?" He shrugged.

"Yes, there's a problem with that," Janet said.

But Gigi was now hanging on to Ricky's leg, and he was bending to kiss her head and reaching into his bag to pull out Sweet 16 Barbie, which Gigi had been haranguing Janet about for weeks.

"Of course," Janet said. "Typical."

Gigi began to squeal and jump around the room, stopping only to introduce Barbie and headless Ken to Sweet 16.

"Ricky, this is René," Janet said, pointing at her. "She lives here now."

"Great," Ricky said, like he could give a shit. "I brought you something," he said to Janet. "I didn't forget you." And he reached into his bag again and pulled out a video tape with two blondes on the cover, both kneeling on a bed in skimpy underwear, bursting out of their bras as they leaned forward to kiss each other with exaggerated open mouths.

"Good God, Ricky," Janet said, turning to walk away. "I wish you'd get a life."

Ricky put his suitcase in Janet's bedroom, and when Gigi was asleep, Janet made popcorn and the three of them sat in front of the TV to watch the porno.

They watched about fifteen minutes—René agog, brainless, overwhelmed by the body parts, the various arrangements—before Janet suddenly stood up.

"Enough," she said. "Jesus Christ. Doesn't anybody know anything about anything?"

"What's she talking about?" Ricky countered, turning to René and gesturing to the screen, where a man was mounting one woman, sucking the nipples of another. "I think they know enough. Right? Maybe I'm wrong. Maybe I don't know shit." He laughed.

"There," Janet said. "You finally hit the nail on the head, Ricky. You finally got it. I'm going to bed."

So Janet left the room, and Ricky and René sat for a few tense moments before Ricky finally said, "Better get my ass in there. Now or never." And he bounced off the sofa. "Want me to turn this off?"

He didn't wait for René to answer. He just took the movie out of the player, waved good night, and disappeared into Janet's bedroom.

Ricky stayed around for the whole week—Janet cooking and cleaning, the two of them taking Gigi to the zoo and the toy store.

"He's okay," Janet said the next Saturday after Ricky had left—driving off as Janet and René waved after him and Gigi wailed. "But I can't really say I'm sorry to see him go." Which both was and wasn't hard to understand.

So René was once again on the floor with Gigi playing Barbies—now with a Sweet 16 Barbie, a camper, a swimming pool, a lounge chair, a picnic table, plus a new Ken with an attached head.

And since Barbie and the new Ken could now kiss without Ken's head falling off, they tended to leave headless Ken out of it—either packing him away in Gigi's new Barbie case or simply throwing him under the couch. They'd dig him out in an emergency—like when the two Barbies had to go on a double date, or when the Barbies were fighting over which one the good Ken was really in love with—but he didn't add much. And it wouldn't be long before they were snapping him back into the case or pitching him sideways, happy enough to just forget about him.

56

"Can you mail it to me?" René said as the school counselor looked her over, aghast.

"Are you sure? It's a special day, you know. I'm guessing your parents would like to see you—"

"Positive." The last thing René needed was another go-around with Eve and Al.

So the counselor gathered the necessary paperwork, and René filled out the forms to have her high school diploma mailed directly to South Dakota, not that she was going to be there to receive it. If things went according to plan—fingers crossed—by the time it arrived, she'd already be in New York.

ISN'T IT TIME TO GET WHAT YOU WANT?

She took a tab from the flyer tacked up in the school library. And the next weekend she drove out past the suburbs, into the foothills, finally turning down a long gravel road that led to a big white house with matching picket fences zigzagging into the distance. The rolling hills were filled with pine and aspen, leaves sparkling in the sunlight. A row of blue spruce lined the driveway like sentinels.

There was a small carriage house in the back where the course advertised in the flyer—promising "a simple ancient secret to make your every dream come true"—was taking place. She parked her car and knocked at the door.

A guy named Kurt answered, saying, "Why's this thing shut, anyway?"

Kurt was rail thin, with light gray eyes and a sweet, wistful expression. And as René complimented the house, the rolling hills, he laughed, saying that he was just the groundskeeper, that he'd come here a few years ago, after dropping out of college. He smiled and led her into a small room where folks were sitting cross-legged on the floor—all chatting and joking, most around Kurt's age.

Kurt pointed out a place for her to sit, then went to the front and knelt down solemnly. The room quieted as he lit a stick of incense, waving it over his head. He placed the incense in a carved wooden holder on a low table set up with a small bowl of water, a dish of fruit, and a candle, all at the base of a black lacquered box hanging upright on the wall. Pressing his palms together, he intoned something incomprehensible, and slowly, deliberately, he opened the box to reveal a scroll covered in decorative Eastern calligraphy. Then he sounded a gong and looked out over the few who were gathered.

"Imagine," Kurt started, "getting everything you ever wanted, everything you've ever dreamed of."

He was easy and likable.

"And the best part—am I right? It's not religion. It's science. Proven. So you don't have to believe in it. You just have to do it."

The others, who'd clearly heard all this before, were captured.

"Say you've been thinking about a new car—some shiny blue truck or little red convertible—and suddenly there it is, pulling up beside you. *Your* car! So you think, 'Why can't *I* have a car like that? Why do *I* have to drive this old piece of junk?'"

People laughed softly, knowingly, while René wondered at all the old cars lined up in the carriage house driveway. But maybe it was a process.

"Well, today—right now—you're the lucky ones," Kurt said, and he recited what he called the "magic formula," going step-by-step through a rhythmic six-syllable chant, saying it over and over as the group picked up speed. Then he stopped.

"I want you to close your eyes, look inside, and think of all the things you've ever wanted. Think of having everything you want right now. Think of having it right here beside you. *Yours*. Whatever you have in mind—decide on it, chant for it. When I ring the gong, keep your eyes closed and we'll all chant together, just like we practiced. And when I ring the gong a second time, you can open your eyes."

He rang the gong.

René joined in the chanting, sometimes opening her eyes to check on the darkened room, the scroll, the group, all earnestly reciting. But she was having trouble figuring out what to chant for. With her eyes closed, looking inward like Kurt had instructed, things were diffuse and shifting, everything so mixed up she couldn't locate a source: Did she want to dance? *Yes, but not like this. Not all sloppy and half-assed. Not with Dicker.* Did she want to go back home? *No, definitely not, but sort of. Maybe if things were different there.* Did she want a boyfriend?

The previous weekend she'd spent the whole afternoon walking Janet's neighborhood, talking to the early daffodils and barely leafing trees, her mind overcome with longing. It was finally spring. With the snowpack melted away, the trees were beginning to blossom—hard buds forming at the ends of branches, here and there a fragrant bloom exploding into light. She'd stopped to admire an enormous cottonwood, patting its bark, looking up the length of it—its knotted trunk leading to something wild, spread open, etched against the sky like a nerve ending—and wished with all her might that there was someone with her, standing beside her.

How different it would have been if only Dan had waited for her to return from Christmas, or Marcus had found the courage to break with Dicker, or Jim Davis had actually chosen her instead of merely undressing her. She could have been riding the pastures in Dan's pickup, or standing with Marcus at the barre, helping him with technique, or smiling secretly at Jim Davis in the hallways, anticipating yet another blissful afternoon at his place. And how different going home would be if only she and Eve could talk about things and laugh together, if only they could be like friends instead of quarreling all the time.

Still, there had to be someone—someone who wanted her, someone who wanted to hold her hand, to kiss her deeply, like Marcus had done, someone who wouldn't dream of humiliating her the way Jim Davis had, telling her to go away, to stop calling, even though he'd been more than happy to lay her on his bed and run his hands over every inch of her naked body.

But since there seemed to be no one—and she couldn't just stand there all day with her palms pressed against that tree trunk—she'd walked on, peering into the windows of the houses she passed, wondering if maybe there wasn't someone inside, just as lonely, looking out at her.

She kept her eyes shut tight, reciting the syllables.

In the darkness behind her closed eyelids, she was an orphan sent away to complete a trial. If she succeeded, there'd be love and celebration. If not, there'd be disappointment and humiliation. So what did she want?

She didn't want to live on the edge of a sharp blade like that anymore. She didn't want to feel so alone. With or without her, life was moving forward—and she didn't want to be left behind. She wanted someone to like her—*just because*—someone to want her around—*just because*.

She wanted a boyfriend. She wanted a boyfriend. She wanted a boyfriend. *Now.*

57

THE CHANTERS WANTED TO SHARE ABOUT THEIR experiences, piping up to tell about things they'd gotten for themselves by chanting—new hiking boots, a mountain bike. Then they all decided to hit the Ramada down the road, just before the turnoff to the highway, and have a drink.

Kurt came up and put a hand on René's arm, saying he hoped she'd be back for the midweek session. "We're a nice group," he added. "We like to have a good time. You should come out with us. It'll be fun."

So she followed Kurt's car out of the driveway, and went with the others through an unlit side door of the Parkway Ramada Lounge.

They sat near the piano, where a man was playing requests. When the waiter came over, asking for ID, René ordered a club soda. Then Kurt ordered two brandies, warmed. "All for me," he said slyly, winking at her.

The waiter came back with two snifters on a tray, setting

the brandies alight as the table whistled and hooted. After the waiter had snuffed them out and placed them on the table, Kurt quietly slid one over to René, shrugging at her as the guys in the group told dirty jokes and the women called out tunes for the piano player.

And when most of the others had left, Kurt turned to her.

"You should come back to the house," he said. "It's a nice night. And there's a swimming pool. Did you see it?"

René had seen the pool glistening between the main house and Kurt's carriage house when she'd first pulled in. After their second round of brandies, she and Kurt had started leaning into each other, his arm settling on the back of her chair. But she tilted her head, declining.

He leaned closer. "You can follow me. I won't lose you. Promise."

Kurt was a nice guy—spiritual and sincere. Everyone in the group looked up to him. And he obviously liked René—ordering her drinks, looking out for her. So maybe she shouldn't be so "uptight," like Janet always said. Maybe she needed to "loosen up." Maybe this was just what she'd been chanting for. Maybe it was already working.

58

When she pulled up to the carriage house, in the dark this time, the air was crisp and the crickets were singing. Kurt took her hand and led her to the swimming pool.

"Looks good, right?"

She sat at the edge, letting her legs dangle in the water.

"I don't have a suit," she said, turning to him. "Guess we have to skinny dip."

He laughed, standing close behind her.

"I've heard about girls like you, you know. Little high school girls who do all kinds of things."

She looked away then, puzzled, thinking about all those girls—Jim Davis's new girlfriend, who hadn't been a virgin since she was in the eighth grade, Dan's ugly yellow-haired girl now riding in the front seat of his pickup.

She'd certainly fallen behind those Phoenix girls in her ballet training. Was she going to fall behind all the other girls, too—the regular ones who were busy preparing themselves, gathering information and experience, fashioning themselves into grown-up women? Was she planning to be a virgin forever?

"Turn your back," she said. And she sprang up and ran to the far side of the pool to strip down. From the dim outdoor light of the carriage house she could see that Kurt was stripping down, too, unzipping his pants, pulling his shirt over his head.

She dove in, Kurt jumped in after, and in just a few strokes he had her in his arms.

59

He led her, naked, into his bedroom, at the opposite end of the carriage house from where they'd done the chanting, and pushed her gently down onto his bed. She tried to pull the sheets up, but he pulled them back, uncovering her, running his hands over her hips and legs, kissing her neck and chest until he was suddenly up on his knees, rolling on a condom.

After that, no matter how she moved or how he angled himself, it was like she was some kind of molded plastic doll, missing the necessary parts.

Since nothing was working, Kurt turned onto his back and told her to get on top.

"This way. Like this," he said. "There. Like that."

When that didn't work, either, he simply stopped, holding her firmly by the hips as she straddled him. "Wait a minute," he said, looking at her completely for maybe the first time all night. "Have you not done this before?"

René shook her head, angry at herself for not being able to manage, as Eve would say, "even the simplest thing."

"*What?*" he said, pushing her off him, moving her to the far side of his big bed. "Holy shit. What the hell? Fuck."

She lay on her back and watched as he raised a hand to his head. For a moment she thought he was going to tell her to go home, like Jim Davis had done. Instead, he climbed back on top of her, fiercely this time, and guided himself into her, *hard,* ignoring the fact that her body was clearly dead set against the idea.

Kurt gave three sharp thrusts, let out a plaintive groan, and pulled out. "Shit," he said. "Jesus Christ." Then he jumped up, sprinted off to the bathroom, and came back as she lay clutching between her legs, startled, breathless, wondering what had just happened. But before she could pull herself together, he was on top of her again, doing the same thing, exactly—crying out, "Shit. No," then moaning and falling onto her with his full weight.

She felt only stabbing pain as he entered her, followed by numb confusion on his retreat. There was none of the thrill Janet had described, none of the ecstasy she'd seen in Ricky's porno movie, none of the simple urgency she'd felt with Marcus or Jim Davis, not even the general yearning she'd had with Dan.

He went away again and came back saying, "Jesus Christ, girl. What're you doing to me?" Then he climaxed just as quickly and hurried off.

It was unnerving to watch Kurt going through whatever he was going through—running off to the bathroom to switch condoms, then coming back again and again. It was indecipherable—like trying to make sense of that foreign chant, or like waking up in a dark room you'd never seen before but knew you didn't belong in, leaving you searching for the smallest sliver of light.

Still, when Kurt was finally lying quietly beside her, René turned and put her hand on his chest, swinging her long leg across his body, like a girl in a movie about people in love. He took her hand, holding it as he turned away. And as he fell asleep, she folded herself against his back, bending every part of herself to fit into him—noticing, mainly, that he was still holding her hand.

60

With the sun hovering just above the horizon, spreading feathery gray light through the early-morning mist, René finally pulled back into Janet's driveway.

"Where the *hell* were you?" Janet cried when René first stepped through the door. She was red-faced, furious, pacing, acting like René's own mother. "Why didn't you call me? Jesus Christ, René. I thought you were dead!"

When René told her that she'd finally done it—she'd had *sex* and now she had a *boyfriend*!—Janet just screamed even louder. "For Christ sakes, René. What the *hell* are you doing? What are you *thinking*? You don't even *know* this guy. It's *outrageous*!" Then she stomped off to her bedroom, slamming the door.

So René sat mute at the kitchen table, helping herself to the Apple Jacks Gigi was also eating right out of the box, thinking that it didn't matter what Janet said. She was with Kurt now. So it was none of Janet's business.

On Wednesday she skipped Dicker's class and drove out to the carriage house. Kurt wasn't there, so one of the women took over the meeting—lighting the incense and ringing the gong. And afterward they all went out to the Ramada.

Sam—who was older than the others, plus overweight and prematurely bald—sat next to her, trying to put his arm around her like Kurt had done, but she scooted away. And when he asked if she wanted a drink, she just pointed to her club soda.

"What'sa matter?" he said. "I do somethin' wrong?"

"Sorry," she said. "I'm with Kurt."

Sam's face lit up and he rocked back in his chair. "You're not with Kurt. Jesus, kid. Kurt's got a girlfriend. Same girl since they both moved here from Idaho like three years ago. You didn't know? I think they grew up next door to each other on neighboring potato farms or some shit."

Sam told her the girl was away, visiting her mother, that Kurt was with her, which was why he was gone. He said they'd be back, that if she didn't believe him she could come to chanting on Saturday. They'd be there. Kurt's girl had a big Movado watch Kurt had given her with a diamond on the twelve—like they were engaged, but not really. René could just look for it. She'd see it. That was Kurt's girl.

Sam was obviously drunk.

"You can always come home with me," he concluded, leaning over.

"I have to go," René said, getting up.

"I'll go with ya."

"No," she said firmly. But Sam stood up and followed her outside.

He stumbled drunkenly behind her through the dark parking lot, and when she got to her car door, he lunged forward, trying to get a hand on her. She quickly stepped aside—causing him to fall onto the hood of her car. So she jumped in, locked her door, and started the engine—Sam banging on her window, cursing as she pulled away, then running for his truck.

On the highway—with Sam right behind her—she tried to think of where to go. If she went to Janet's, he'd know where she lived. So she drove as fast as she could, trying to come up with a safe location and at the same time trying to ditch him.

She hit eighty, eighty-five, but he stayed with her, pulling up alongside her, calling out his window, waving and laughing, like they were playing drag race. Suddenly the exit to Janet's was next and, in the darkness, all three freeway lanes were empty. She stayed in the middle, accelerating—her speedometer topping ninety, ninety-three—with Sam still in the far left, pulling ahead and dropping behind. If she could keep her speed up until just a split second before the exit, he'd be going too fast to get over. So she stayed in the middle, continuing to accelerate, and at the last possible moment—with zero warning—she dodged across two lanes, caught the exit, and left Sam sailing off into the night.

Sam blew his horn and slammed on his brakes, and she drove as fast as she could to Janet's house, where she parked and ran inside.

The next Saturday she went back to the carriage house. She had to see Kurt, to find out what was going on. Sam wasn't around, but the girl Sam had told her about, with the Movado watch, was sitting up in front. Kurt nodded at René from across the room. And when the chanting was finished, he came up and told her that Sam said he was sorry, that he hadn't meant to scare her.

"I'm not worried about Sam," she said, though she was relieved he wasn't there. "What about you?"

"What?" Kurt said, just like he'd said it that night in bed. *What?* "I hope I didn't give you the wrong impression."

Then the girl with the Movado came over and put her arm around Kurt's waist. And Kurt draped his arm over her shoulders, giving her a quick kiss, and introduced them.

61

RICKY WAS CALLING EVERY DAY, BEGGING JANET to bring their daughter and come visit him over the summer.

"Texas?" René heard Janet screaming into the phone. "Are you out of your mind, Ricky? Jesus. It's a hundred and ten degrees down there. No way."

Janet had started having Paulo, the new foreign-exchange student from her English class, over to the house—at first for tutoring, though now the two of them were spending most of their time in Janet's bedroom with the door closed. Paulo was staying in town for the summer, so Janet wasn't going anywhere.

Dicker was out of his neck brace and back to walking the length of the studio, studying himself in the mirror. He and Marcus had obviously made their amends, though Dicker wasn't taking it any easier on him and Marcus wasn't getting the least bit better at ballet.

And—though she never returned to the group—as Kurt's ancient rhyming chant swam in her head, René found that there was only one thing she truly wanted. She wanted *out*.

Out, out, out. Out of Dicker's ridiculous classes; out of thinking about Kurt and his snap-on, snap-off condoms and secret Movado girlfriend; out of the stinging humiliation of Jim Davis; out of the sneaking suspicion that Marcus might have really loved her; out of Janet's baroque family drama; out of Denver. *Out.* Period.

A note arrived from Eve:

We're all doing good. Leon's got a job delivering Pepsi to local gas stations and seems to be keeping out of trouble. All his friends have moved away, so that's likely for the best. Dad's gone, and Jayne's out and about, running around the neighborhood, already in shorts though it's still too cold. Everyone's hoping for a change in the weather.

Mrs. G's found a friend of a friend in New York. She's supposed to be a nice lady so maybe she can help find a place for you to stay when you get there. I'm going to write to her and see what she says.

So that was all they would have to go on—a friend of a friend of her old teacher Mrs. G. No recommended places for her to study, no specific teachers for her to meet, no special introductions. She'd be going to New York with nothing— more like a tourist than a serious ballet dancer.

Who knows? the letter went on. *Just have to wait and see. Que será será.*

René folded the letter and stuck it back in the envelope, bending to place it by her bed with one hand pressed against her stomach like she was covering a stab wound. Then she went out to Janet's front porch, to look out at the sky and collect herself.

If Denver had taught her anything, it was that even her truncated time with her family was at an end, and—if Kurt and the others were any clue—there wasn't going to be anyone stepping in to fill the gap.

She had to prepare to move on to New York, where she'd get a chance to start over and maybe do it right this time. Though she understood that she wasn't ready—just a few weeks ago someone walking behind her into the ballet studio had called out "Heather!," mistaking her for one of Dicker's misshapen oddball students—still, it was time to go.

She'd lost her way in Denver. She'd been stupid—wasting her time, committing every possible sin for a girl her age: sloth, fornication, drunkenness, anger. Everyone she knew was mad at her and she was mad at everyone right back. Of course she knew better. She knew what was waiting for sinners, for those who didn't "measure up," as Eve said it.

So was she ever going to "make something of herself"? Was she going to be able to accomplish even the least of what she'd been sent away from home to do? Was she going to become what they expected her to become, what she expected of herself—to lift them up, to make them all happy and proud? And was *that* what she wanted? Did she even believe in those things anymore?

At least she could finally leave this place. She could work hard and catch up once she got to New York. She could do that much, couldn't she?

She sat on Janet's front steps, looking off into the distance like she was trying to see into the future. Pale white butterflies were flitting atop the weeds now blossoming in Janet's front yard. And though it sometimes seemed that they were falling—flapping, tumbling end over end—they were simply *flying,* diving down and coming up again. Which is what she'd been doing, too, she figured—just beating her way through the air, like everyone else.

New York, she thought, taking a deep breath, gathering herself. *New York. Ready or not.*

NEW YORK CITY, 1975

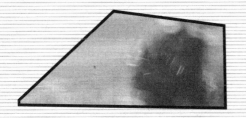

Ready or Not

62

They'd each brought a suitcase, though Eve's was packed mainly with things she planned to leave behind, things she thought René would likely find useful in the long run—a kitchen towel, a potholder, a sewing kit with spare buttons, along with knitted wool slippers she'd washed then felted in the dryer.

They picked up their luggage at baggage claim and joined the flood of travelers, watching for signs to buses into Manhattan. Relieved to see a policeman leaning against a railing near the exit, Eve stopped to ask for directions. But he just waved her on like she was being a nuisance, holding everything up. "Up ahead, lady. Keep moving."

They needed to get to Penn Station or Grand Central. Eve didn't know which. It looked like either one would get them close enough to St. Mary's Residence, that from either they could walk or at least afford to take a cab.

The suitcases were heavy and it was sweltering—muggy and close. They followed the signs to ground transportation, then got stuck in a taxi line and had to backtrack until they spotted a sign with a picture of a bus and below it, simply enough—MIDTOWN.

Eve turned to René. "Looks like this is it," she said, putting down her suitcase. She stepped back to get out of the choking fumes.

"You sure?"

"About as sure as I can be. I don't see anything else that looks just right. Do you?" There were signs for trains to Far Rockaway, buses to New Jersey, Queens, the Bronx. "It's got to be this one." But Eve wasn't sure. "Soon as it gets here, we can hop on and ask."

So they joined the loosely formed line, and when the bus finally arrived—brakes squealing, doors opening with a heavy moan—they jostled forward with the others, pushing onto the steps.

Eve bent to ask the driver about their stop, and not even looking up, he bellowed, "Penn Station. Grand Central. Take your pick."

"Hallelujah," she said, turning to René.

And just as they found two open seats near the back, the bus took off.

The other passengers were settling in—fanning themselves with airline tickets or crumpled magazines, some letting their heads fall against the dirty windows—but Eve and René sat upright, marveling at the weaving, barking taxis, the freeways circling up and over their heads as the bus careened through one crumbling overpass after the next, each covered in swirling graffiti and missing great chunks of concrete. And suddenly out the windows on either side were miles and miles of slanting gravestones, twisting up out of the earth like overcrowded teeth, stretching on for as far as the eye could see.

"Just like right here in life," Eve noted. "Not a breath of air between them."

She shook her head, galled on behalf of all those dead people lined up one against the next. And they rode in silence, each contemplating the great multitude of lives that had been lived in this place, the vast numbers, the haunting variety all come to occupy the same ground.

They pointed out one thing after the next to each other as they bumped along in the river of cars, which were dodging in and out, not minding the lanes or the rules, each one weaving full throttle on the pitted, worn-out roads, looking for an advantage.

"And just look at those houses," Eve said. "Good grief."

There were more little houses all set in a row than either of them had ever seen in their lives, all in dingy pastels, looking like something out of a storybook—narrow façades, peaked roofs, small railed porches—one house hanging on to the next with no yard, no grass, just a few scrappy trees coming up out of the concrete here and there, their scrawny brown leaves trembling though there wasn't the least wisp of air.

"Those trees could certainly use some TLC," Eve said bitterly, blaming she didn't know who, but somebody. Somebody knew better than that.

"Is this it, do you think?" René asked.

"I don't think so. I think we'll know it when we see it."

And suddenly, as if speaking had the power to conjure, there it was: New York City, coming into view—skyscrapers gleaming in the sunlight, domes, arcs, needles, mirrored boxy squares all overlapping to form a jagged, burning line in the distance, and majestic bridges, each as perfect as a scale model, spanning the approaching stretch of water. They gasped, dazzled. But before they could take it all in, they were barreling underground, speeding through a long dark tunnel.

"This is going to be something," Eve said, straining for the tunnel's end.

Finally a pinpoint of light appeared and began to grow. And they emerged into stark daylight, as if being born into this new place, to find themselves surrounded by soaring elevations of brick and concrete.

"Like being in a canyon," René said.

"I think we can safely say this is it. That's for sure."

"You can't even see the sky. Only a sliver."

René leaned this way and that, attempting to catch a slice of open horizon at the far end of each of the long rows of buildings—whatever sunlight there was now stymied by concrete.

"Your new home," Eve said, patting René's leg nervously. In just a few days Eve would be leaving, going back to South Dakota. "I wish I could stay with you."

"Me, too," René said. She couldn't even think about being left behind here by herself. If she thought about it, she might cry. So she put it out of her mind and searched, street after street, for that slice of sunlight, that promise that the wide blue sky—even if hidden from sight—was still up there somewhere, arching above her.

63

EVE UNFOLDED HER MAP, TURNING IT ONE WAY and the other, trying to figure out where they were. She couldn't make heads or tails of it until the bus finally stopped and the driver called out, "Penn Station!"

"Got it," Eve said, circling the spot. "Let's stay on. If I'm not completely turned around—" She shifted her map, holding it at an angle. "Grand Central should be closer."

So they stayed put as others shuffled off the bus.

"Looks like there's another stop, too," Eve went on. "Even higher up."

The bus was taking off, leaving Penn Station behind.

"I think— If I'm not wrong—" Eve was crimping her map into sections, frantically trying to match it up to the bus route.

"Let's get off at the next one," René said, starting to panic about where they might actually end up. "Look. We're here."

After just a few short blocks the bus had stopped again.

Without making the usual announcement about where they were, the bus driver opened the doors—the mechanical moan now lost to a percussive racket coming from the street—

and took off down the steps. So René pushed up the aisle, leaned out the door, and called after him, "Grand Central?"

He looked her up and down and almost laughed.

"You want Grand Central, honey?" He pointed down the street—beyond the men with jackhammers and yellow vests, past the flood of pedestrians rushing around them—to an enormous building, the breadth of which made an undeniable T, blocking both cars and pedestrians just a few intersections ahead. "You got it, sweetheart."

"Here!" she called back to Eve, ignoring all the people now pushing past her. "We're here, Mom! Come on. Let's go!"

So Eve folded up her map, gathered her purse, grabbed her carry-on, then squeezed out of her seat and into the line of folks getting off the bus as René waited on the sidewalk, watching a group of jockey-like men form a random perimeter around the activity of the arriving passengers.

"Taxi, taxi! Taxi here!" the men kept yelling, shouting over one another as the bus driver—who looked to be standing guard, keeping his large body between the men and the suitcases he was unloading—shooed them away.

"We need a taxi," René called when she saw Eve coming off the steps.

One of the men jumped forward. "Which one's your bags? This one? This one?" He pointed from a distance at the suitcases now lined up on the pavement. The bus driver scowled, glancing back at René, shaking his head, irritated and fed up. With what? These men? This crazy city?

René confirmed their bags, and the small man stepped in and grabbed them, one in each hand, saying, "Follow, follow. Come. I find you taxi."

"What's going on?" Eve said, boxed in by the crush of people suddenly pushing and shoving around the unloaded luggage.

"He's getting us a taxi!" René called, pointing to the man, who'd already started down the street at a clip, snaking his way through the onslaught of pedestrians.

"What in the world?" Eve shouted as René took off after him.

"They walk fast here, Mom! Hurry!" René called over her shoulder as Eve stumbled along behind, holding tightly to her purse and carry-on. "Excuse me, excuse me," René could hear her saying to nearly everyone she passed.

The little man was darting through the crowd, speed-walking through red lights and flashing DO NOT WALK signs, going faster and faster. So René picked up the pace, nearly jogging to keep up with him, glancing back every few feet to keep track of Eve, who was falling farther and farther behind.

She couldn't lose their suitcases, but she also couldn't lose Eve. So she ran, looking backward and forward at the same time, for once feeling lucky that the suitcase her grandmother had given her all those years ago when she'd first left home was neon yellow. It stuck out. When she lost track of the little man, she just had to watch for that flash of color, knee level in the crowd.

The man ran three blocks, crossed through traffic to Grand Central, turned left, tore down Forty-second Street, and finally dropped their bags at the corner, in front of a waiting cab, with René just a few lengths behind. She caught up, and as they waited together for Eve—the runner bent and gasping, René winded—the taxi driver got out, slammed his door, gave the man hell in a language René couldn't understand, then picked up their bags and tossed them in the trunk.

Eve showed up disheveled, red-faced and huffing.

"Taxi. I get for you," the running man said to her, bowing like a liveryman attending a horse-drawn carriage. He was dripping sweat. And it was then René noticed that, despite the oppressive heat, the man who'd carried their suitcases all this way had on a ripped down jacket with dirty feathers sticking out, over a torn, moth-eaten sweater.

"Well, what in the world," Eve said to him, trying to smooth back her hair as the man held out his hand. "I've never heard of such a thing."

"I carry for you," the man insisted. "I carry so far. I find you taxi. You tip."

Eve shook her head, grumbling, but she opened her purse. She rummaged around and handed him two quarters.

"So?" the man said, raising his over-padded arms at her. "All this and so nothing? Not worth."

"Well, I'm sorry, but—"

"You give more!"

René was already in the cab.

"That's all," Eve said, waving the running man away. "That's it."

Eve got in the cab, pulling her door shut. And as the man hollered, making obscene gestures in her direction, she leaned forward and gave the address of St. Mary's—the Upper East Side women's residence the friend of a friend of Mrs. G's had, in response to Eve's letter, written to suggest they try.

64

THEY SPENT THE ENTIRE CAB RIDE GETTING A lecture from the driver.

That guy who'd offered to carry their bags was planning to rob them, he said. It was the oldest trick in town. He even wanted the cabbie to go in on it—to take their bags and drive off before the two of them could catch up.

"Well, I knew something was out of whack," Eve huffed. "Lesson number one," she said to René.

"If those suitcases were a little lighter, lady, they'd be long gone. You'd never see those bags again. And you— You tipped him!" The cabdriver snorted. "He was trying to take everything you had, and you, lady, you gave him a tip!"

"Well, I never thought—"

"Better get used to it," the cabbie scolded. "You're in the big city now, miss. Anything's possible. Any bad thing you can imagine, here it is."

He left it at that. And when they pulled up in front of St. Mary's, Eve paid him, handing him two shiny extra quarters.

"You're gonna give me the same you give him? That guy

who was stealing all your earthly belongings?" The cabdriver set their bags on the sidewalk. "You think that's fair?"

"Well, thank you," Eve tried, standing close over their luggage now as the driver got back into his cab, giving her the stink eye.

"You better watch out, miss," he called. "Better open your eyes." Then he turned on his light and took off.

Eve and René looked at each other. Eve shook her head, finally putting her coin purse away. "I don't know why in the *sam* hell he'd want to get after *me* about it," she said.

But they were relieved. It was quieter on this street, and they were happy to see the statue of the Virgin Mary up high, arms open, as if to welcome them.

They carried their suitcases up the steps to the locked front doors of St. Mary's Residence and peered through the glass into the small lobby with its decorative tile and wooden benches.

"Finally," Eve said, sighing as if everything she'd ever dreamed of had already come true. "We're here."

Then she reached up and shouted their names through the intercom. And they stood on Seventy-second Street, just a few steps off the pavement, waiting for someone at St. Mary's to come open the door.

65

St. Mary's was on the Upper East Side, which was relatively clean even though nearly every block of New York City had dog shit on the sidewalks and garbage stacked into towers on the curbs, loose trash blowing in the wind, rats dodging in and out in open daylight. Local newspapers across the country ran pictures of cars on fire in the streets of Manhattan, kids with nowhere to play running bases in Brooklyn traffic, fire hydrants turned loose in the Bronx so that people could splash in the gutters. Parks all over the city were littered with needles and passed-out addicts. There were shoot-outs and drug busts, dismembered mobsters stuffed into trash bins. In Central Park, it seemed that girls were being raped and murdered with numbing regularity.

And even without all of that, New York wasn't any ordinary kind of place.

Eve had done everything she could with long-distance phone calls and a notepad—gotten René to the city, found her a place to live. But once they were through the airport, to the bus, to the cab, then up the steps to St. Mary's and installed in their rooms, her planning hit a dead end.

"The best I can figure," she said to René, "is that, come morning, we look up ballet companies and dance schools in the Yellow Pages and just go for a visit. What do you say?"

"Okay," René said. "But will they let us in?"

"I don't know why not."

They were in St. Mary's tenth-floor communal kitchen/living room, which had a mini-fridge, a hot plate, a few pots and pans, a little television.

Earlier that night—while René had waited in the lobby, pacing, searching through the glass—Eve had ventured out onto the dark streets, returning as triumphant as a big-game hunter, with eggs, butter, crackers, cheese, bread, jam.

"It's so nice out there. Really, René," she'd said coming through the glass doors. "Nothing to be afraid of. You should've come with me. You definitely missed out." She sighed, her airy tone making it clear that, though she'd spent her entire life on the dusty plains of South Dakota, Eve herself was ready for anything.

"This common area will be a nice spot for you to meet people," she said now, cranking up her enthusiasm as a counterweight to the strikingly downtrodden appearance of the tenth-floor living room, which was more like a doctor's office waiting room—with hard plastic chairs and out-of-date, dog-eared magazines.

She was standing at the little kitchen counter, marking the groceries she'd secured with René's name and room number.

"If you ever get lonely, just bring a book and hang out in here. I bet you'll meet lots of new friends."

If I ever get lonely? René thought, wondering what her own mother could possibly imagine her life had been like for the past few years.

As if on cue, a stooped-over old lady in a food-stained housedress shuffled in and took a cold chicken leg from the icebox. Eve tried to start a conversation—to introduce René and tell the lady that René was going to be living here, too—but the lady only grimaced, shying away, then bobbed her head a few times and scurried out of the room.

"I'm sure they're not all like that," Eve whispered as René blanched.

And they sat on the plastic couch to eat their scrambled eggs.

In the morning they'd go to the pay phone in the hall—which had a local New York phone book chained to the counter—and make a list of ballet companies and schools.

"Might as well get started," Eve said. "We're not going to have forever to get this figured out. But maybe we can find time to see some sights while I'm here. Like the Empire State Building or the Statue of Liberty. Wouldn't that be fun?"

They washed up the dishes, and after following Eve to Eve's room to say good night, René went down the hall to her own room, shutting the metal fire door behind her and locking herself in. She pulled out her little daybed—which took up the entire width of the small room, from one side to the other, making it impossible for her to stand. So she climbed over the bed to the foot end, where there was a single window, thinking that Eve was right, that she should at least look out and see where she was.

But when she lifted the shade—expecting to see the street, to watch all the people below walking in the night—she was faced, instead, with a solid brick wall directly on the other side of the glass. If she could have forced that window open, she could have reached out and touched it.

She sat for a minute, studying the blank brick wall, following the water marks that ran down its face in subtle trails of discoloration, like dried tears. Then she lowered the shade and fell back onto her bed, her body taking up nearly the full length of the room—her "new home," as Eve kept calling it.

And as she lay staring at the ceiling, she was grateful that Eve was still just down the hall. Maybe after a few days here Eve would see that, for René, this wasn't going to be anything like a holiday. Maybe, just maybe, this small taste of René's life would help Eve to realize that this hadn't been some walk in the park—not for a minute—and that, even now, no matter how hard Rene tried, all the hopes and dreams they'd had for her might end up coming to nothing.

With Eve's expectations adjusted and realigned, René would finally be free to either succeed or to fail, without the need of a win so big it redeemed everyone and everything, or the fear of a loss so deep it destroyed not only her own dreams but the dreams of everyone who cared about her.

But she was tired. She could hear Eve's voice in her head. Eve could have been right there in the room with her or ten thousand miles away. *You're just tired. Go lie down and close your eyes.*

Eve had said it back when René was little and crying over a splinter, and she'd said it whenever René had called home from Phoenix or Denver—too often exhausted and discouraged.

"You're just tired. Go lie down. It'll all look better in the morning."

So she closed her eyes—her mind running rapidly from where she'd first started to where she was now—all at once realizing that *yes,* she was finally *here,* in this city of cities, the center of it all. And she began to feel a surge of something like happiness, even elation, rising in her, welling up. She was surprised to find herself—lying there with her hands behind her head, eyes now wide open—nearly smiling.

She was in *New York,* after all. After all this time, after all that had happened along the way, this was going to be her chance. And—in spite of her lack of prospects, her downtrodden quarters, her bedroom hovel—she was excited.

After the cot with the wooden door across the frame in the corner of Gali's bedroom, after the filthy dangling canopy pom-poms at the Babbitts', after the basement lair at Janet's, she was used to shoddy quarters. Shoddy quarters were nothing. Shoddy quarters were normal.

And despite everything, she'd worked hard. Her old teacher Mrs. G had given her a good start, and back in Phoenix, Mr. B had set her in the right direction. Even through all the ineptitude and distractions she'd found in Denver, she'd held on to what they'd taught her—to her clean technique, to her beautiful line.

In spite of everything, she'd never let go of her training, even as she'd sometimes veered so far off course. And now—*she was here*! In New York City! And she didn't have to do it alone this time. Eve was here to help her. They could do it together.

So she was ready. Given where she'd started from and all she'd been through to get here, she was as ready as she could possibly be.

66

THEY COULD SEE FROM THE ADDRESS IN THE phone book that the Harkness House for Ballet Arts was just a few blocks over and three blocks up. According to Eve's map, all the other ballet schools and companies were either on the far side of Central Park or way downtown. And when Eve grumbled about how costly it was going to be if René ended up having to ride the bus each day, René shot back, "Yes—and exhausting," in a sharp, peevish tone she hadn't intended, recalling Dan racing past her each day at that bus stop in Denver.

"But don't we need to call ahead?" she asked meekly, almost as an apology.

"They're either going to see us or they're not," Eve said. "Might as well just go find out."

So first they were going to Harkness.

Eve stopped for a moment, dropping back into a doorway on Seventy-second Street to double-check her map. And after she'd confirmed that they were walking in the right direction, she folded it up again and surged headlong back into the flow of pedestrians, René right on her heels, her dance bag slung over her shoulder, dodging piles of dog shit.

From the outside, Harkness looked like just another stone building in a row of similar buildings on East Seventy-fifth, but inside, the marble walls, the black-and-white marble floors, the interior Roman columns, the soaring ceilings with pale frescoes of angels romping among purple-blue clouds, all conspired to confirm the orbit between money and beauty, money and elegance, money and aspiration, money and the reflection of the divine. It was money everywhere you looked, telling you everything you needed to know about how God had intended things, each surface radiating refinement, dignity, grace, calm, as if to say that, here, you could finally, once and for all, leave behind not just the noisy city waiting outside your door but all the dirty, useless streets of your past—wherever they were—transcending the fray to join the inner quietude that lay within these burnished walls.

René and Eve were instantly hushed and alert. Though they'd just stepped out of the searing heat—wearing Woolworth zories that barely kept their feet from the burning pavement—they stifled their *ooh*s and *aah*s and did not fan their shirts.

René followed Eve's lead, peering around the corner into the large open area adjoining the foyer. Light was streaming through ceiling-high stained-glass windows, painting the marble in color and shadow, the place apparently empty until, on the far side of that large room, three ballerinas appeared as if out of the ether, hurrying up an enormous curved staircase, not making a sound.

Eve and René continued through the anteroom into the main hall, where they found a door just off to the left that said DIRECTOR.

Eve knocked, and a woman in a trim black skirt and perfect white blouse answered in some amazement of her own. She asked how she might be of help, inviting them in to sit down. And after Eve had explained their purpose—detailing René's previous study as the woman interjected "Marvelous" and "Excellent," always with a stony, listening expression—she went on to narrate the ins and outs of their trip to the city, saying, "A first for the both of us, believe you me!"

The woman nodded politely. Then she reached into a drawer, handing René a form.

"There's class in twenty minutes," she said, checking her watch. "I'll see if the ballet master will let you join as an audition. How does that sound?"

"Oh, ideal," Eve gasped, clasping her hands together.

René nodded, and the lady stood to leave, the click of her heels echoing through the great hall.

"Well, that was lucky," Eve whispered, her eyes wide. "I'll say."

René filled in her name, address, height, weight, birthdate—which she rolled forward by a year so the woman would think she'd just turned sixteen instead of just turned seventeen. It would give her an advantage to be younger. At seventeen she might already be considered a done deal—trained out of any real possibility of dancing. And the closer she got to eighteen, the less anyone was going to be interested in her at all. She tilted the paper to show Eve, pointing to the doctored date.

"Oh, my," Eve said. "Well, let's hope she doesn't ask for a birth certificate."

"Looks like it's your lucky day," the lady said when she got back. "Come with me, René. I'll show you to the dressing room."

So René left Eve sitting on a tufted blue velvet bench outside the office and followed the woman down a narrow back hallway, past what looked like a cafeteria, a lounge, a back studio, another smaller studio—a maze, every turn revealing yet another room with barres, mirrors, a piano.

The woman turned again, and they started down a set of steep concrete steps—the concrete walls on either side plastered with flyers for dance auditions and theater productions—then wound their way through a series of narrow underground corridors to the locker room.

"Here we are. Class is in Studio B," the woman said. Then, likely because of the look on René's face, she added, "Just come back to the office. I'll show you."

And trying not to be rattled by the other girls in the dressing room—each of whom was preparing silently: pinning, tucking, straightening, securing, as if suiting up for combat—René changed as quickly as she could and was back upstairs.

"Top of the stairs," the lady said, pointing both her and Eve to that curved Hollywood staircase.

And turning to the woman, Eve put her hand on her heart

and did something René had never seen her do before. She bowed, as if to a queen. "Thank you," she said.

And they crossed the room and started up the stairway with the intricately carved black railing and shining gold banister, light from the stained glass tinting their bodies as they ascended.

67

STUDIO B HAD SKY-BLUE WALLS WITH INSET GOLD-leaf cameos of garlanded cherubs, mahogany crossbeams on the ceiling—inlaid with so much red, gold, and royal blue they seemed to have come straight from the Vatican—and a fireplace on the back wall with an ornately carved stone mantel of such great breadth and height that four or five dancers could have stood inside without touching an edge.

There were barres along three walls—including the mirrored front wall—but even with three more portable barres set up center-floor, nearly every spot was taken.

Eve found a chair just outside the studio door, and René took a place at one of the barres nearby—in the middle, in case she got lost in the combinations and had to follow.

The dancers warming up around the room wore cut-and-tied plastic warm-up pants pulled up to their chests, leg warmers covering their arms, and leotards cut into deep Vs, back and front, tucked and pinned so that bone, muscle, sinew shone in the mirror. Some had knitted mufflers wrapped around their hips. Almost all had intricate ties and ribbons crisscrossing their arches even in simple ballet slippers. So, in her plain scoop-neck leotard and pink tights, René was noticeably underdressed.

She rolled her feet and stretched her calves self-consciously, copying the movements of the other dancers until the teacher, David Neal, came in and everyone who'd been on the floor—either stretching a leg overhead or sitting in a wide second position, chest planted over split legs—stood.

He stopped to greet some of the dancers, then chatted with the pianist, setting his to-go cup on a small table in the piano alcove. He looked terribly happy, clearly excited about what lay ahead, which—after a whole year of watching Dicker heave a mournful sigh at the start of each class, as if he were once again forced to carry the same dumb load up the same dumb hill—was inspiring.

David Neal clapped twice, and, as the room flooded with glorious, resounding music, the dancers started in on a set warm-up—bending, stretching, turning, leg on the barre, leg off the barre—in unison. René did her best to follow along. Still, she ended up blundering her way through the series, facing the wrong way on the wrong leg, two beats behind, sticking out like a sore thumb. So, not only did she feel naked, standing at the barre without any of the right gear, she felt sluggish and dull next to these lithe, glowing creatures, most of whom, she could see from the warm-up, had extensions up to their ears and straight up-and-down penché arabesques.

Then David Neal took a place at one of the center barres—the dancers around him stepping aside—and demonstrated the first combination, his mastery evident in the lyrical tilt of his head, the crisp, easy extension of his feet. When he'd finished, he nodded to the pianist and the class began in earnest.

And as David Neal—clearly a ballet master to the stars—made his way around the room, he stopped at the door to the studio to ask Eve if she wouldn't rather sit in front, in the small elevated balcony box in the corner, which seemed to be specifically made for viewing.

"Well, that would be lovely," René could hear Eve saying.

So David Neal picked up Eve's chair and, leading her through the lines of working dancers, carried it up the three narrow steps and set it in the balcony box. Then, like the prince in *The Sleeping Beauty*—one hand placed formally behind his back, the other extended toward Eve—he guided and supported her up to her seat.

And as Eve spent the class observing from on high, René worked through the combinations. She could see David Neal glancing her way, keeping his eye on her. And when he finally came and stood just next to her—looking her over without the slightest subterfuge, taking his time—she steeled herself and did not flinch. In the middle of the combination he took her hand, extending her fingers ever so slightly, making her feel elegant and pure, as if it was well within her power to actually belong in a place like this.

"There," he said. "That's right."

And he continued around the room, sometimes quietly observing, sometimes speaking or singing the combinations as they progressed.

68

WHEN CLASS WAS OVER, DAVID NEAL HELPED Eve down from her balcony while René followed the other dancers, hurrying off to the locker room. And when she'd changed and was back upstairs, she found Eve waiting for her on the velvet bench outside the office.

They went in together.

"Well, your timing's excellent," the woman said. She shut the door behind them. "Meaning we just happen to have an opening in the apprentice program. One of the girls was asked to join the company."

She smiled for the first time since they'd come in.

"So I've talked with Mr. Neal, and we're willing to take a chance on you, René, if you're interested."

René and Eve looked at each other in disbelief.

"It doesn't pay more than a bit of spending money. Only a small stipend," the woman warned, apologetic. She set a single page agreement in front of René, already filled out with her name. "And she may need to lose a little weight," the woman added.

"She can do that," Eve said.

"I can do that," René repeated.

The woman explained that René would have to take daily technique classes plus specialty classes in pointe, variation, jazz, modern, depending on the schedule. And on Fridays she could stop by the office to collect her check. There were twelve female and twelve male apprentices. About half were "terminated" every six months in something called "eliminations," she told them. So René would need to work hard if she wanted to stay.

"Perhaps we should talk it over," Eve ventured, looking at René, startled, as though her words were being spoken by someone else. "It's the first place we've visited," she explained.

"That's fine." The woman set down the pen she was just about to hand to René and withdrew the contract. "Let me know in the next few days. And if you have any questions—"

"Of course, we'll be in touch," Eve said coolly.

But once they were back on the street, Eve was ecstatic, gesturing and shouting, "Getting paid instead of paying? Not in my wildest dreams!"

"I should just take it," René tried, thinking she should run back, grab the pen, and sign before some girl who didn't have to "lose a little weight" stepped in and took her place.

"You could. But you never know. You might end up with a better offer. I hate to say it, but it doesn't sound like they have much of a company anymore."

Harkness Ballet—not the least bit profitable and completely dependent on its benefactress, Rebekah Harkness—was no longer in New York City. It had disbanded in the U.S. and been reconfigured in Venezuela, the woman had told them. Only the apprentice program had remained in the States.

"We only stopped at Harkness because it was closest," Eve went on. "But maybe someplace else will give you a better deal. Especially for the long run."

It was a legitimate point.

They went into a diner on Madison Avenue, where Eve had a BLT and coffee while René had cottage cheese with lettuce and tomato.

"How about you choose a place for tomorrow," Eve said.

"We'll go for class, see what happens."

"Maybe the Joffrey?" René had seen a poster for the Joffrey back in Denver when they'd performed at the Civic Center.

"If I remember right, that's *way* downtown," Eve said, her voice filled with sudden trepidation. "Which means bright and early, I guess," she added, reversing course.

Then the waiter came over and handed Eve the check.

"Seventeen dollars for a sandwich?" She scowled at him, shaking her head. "Never in all my life have I paid so much for such a little bit of bacon."

The waiter bent to read the tab, calling out the cost of each item. "Seventeen dollars, twenty-one cents," he said finally.

Eve sighed and took out her wallet. "How does anybody afford to live in this town?" she said to him. "How can anybody get by?"

The waiter cracked a smile. "It ain't easy," he said, nodding.

"I believe that," Eve told him, like they were old friends. "I most certainly do." And she slapped her bills down onto the table, then started digging through her coin purse for the change.

69

When they got back to St. Mary's, Eve double-checked her map, and the next morning—since, after taking ten steps down the dark stairwell to the subway and being struck with the heavy, acrid smell of rancid piss, hot concrete, and engine oil, René turned and ran right back up to the street—they caught the bus and headed downtown.

"Maybe we should've tried somewhere else," Eve said, checking her watch. "Looks like this place is farther away than all the rest put together."

They got off at Twelfth Street and took the long walk across town, finally finding the door to the ballet studio wedged between a dry cleaner and a tattoo parlor. So they hiked up the narrow stairwell—past noisy dancers coming and going—and ended up in a cramped third-floor vestibule looking around for someone to talk to. There was a young girl sitting behind a small desk, stamping passes, so Eve went up to her.

"My daughter's here to see about auditioning," she started.

The girl looked at her, blank.

"Maybe for the training program?" Eve went on. "If there's someone around who could—"

"There's class," the girl said, looking at René. "If she wants to take class."

"Well, sure," Eve said. "But maybe I could talk to one of the teachers."

"The teacher's in class right now," the girl said, indicating a closed door off to one side. "He'll be out soon, though. Maybe ten minutes?"

There was a line forming behind them.

"It's ten dollars for a single," the girl said.

Eve paid the money.

"Well, *this* is a comedown," she muttered hotly to René, as if she'd spent her entire life in places like Harkness and could no longer bear the brutality of the regular world. She told René she'd be sure to talk to the teacher as soon as he came out and that meanwhile René should go ahead and get changed.

The studio was bare-bones—the mirrors water-marked with cracked, brown edges, the floor unevenly stained, dotted with shiny patches of sticky rosin, the tall, dirty windows rattling in their casings every few minutes as trucks rumbled by below. In class, the other dancers were stolid, uninspiring, and René found the combinations rigid and unnatural. She wound up struggling at the barre then floundering in center-floor, the teacher looking right past her. If Eve had spoken to him at all, it was for nothing.

When she came out of the changing room after class—

back in her street clothes—she could see Eve through a glass partition, talking with the teacher. He was gesticulating and shaking his head, finally taking Eve by the arm and leading her back to the girl at the front desk, telling her that the girl would let her know how things worked in terms of tuition and classes.

He turned to leave, and the girl told Eve that she could buy a class card if she wanted a discount. Instead of ten dollars a class, they'd get ten classes for seventy-five dollars.

"No, no, no, no," Eve said as the girl bent to open a bottom drawer. "We just thought—"

The girl shrugged, confused. "No card, then?"

Once again people were lining up behind them, so they stepped out of the way, René turning and Eve following her quickly down the three flights of steps, both thankful to be out on the street again, navigating their way through the crowds.

"Well, that seems clear enough," Eve said bitterly as they hiked back across town.

"The combinations were awful," René put in. "And he didn't even look at me. What the heck?"

As they got on the Third Avenue bus, Eve took out her coin purse. "Plus all these bus fares," she said. "And having to get all the way down here every day. Can you imagine?"

René shook her head, smarting from the teacher's willingness to look past her, and bewildered by her inability to keep up with all those just-plain-ordinary dancers. How could she have been so awkward, so unmusical? Maybe Harkness had been a fluke.

"Should we try someplace else?" Eve asked, clearly cringing at the thought.

René shook her head. She didn't want to try any other place—ever.

"Maybe we should just say yes," Eve suggested. "I could call when we get back. It seems perfect, really. Like somebody up there's looking out for you."

"We should call. Yes. Definitely. Right away."

And for the whole long bus ride back uptown René was agitated—shifting in her seat, groaning at every stop, aggrieved at all the taxis flying past them—worrying over and over that the ballet director at Harkness was going to say she was sorry but the opening in the apprentice program had been filled.

70

BACK AT ST. MARY'S, THEY WENT STRAIGHT TO THE tenth-floor pay phone and Eve dropped in her coins, accepting the position on René's behalf. "Happily," she said.

Then she turned to René. "You can start first thing in the morning—class at ten o'clock. She said to come early and she'll give you a locker."

René heaved a sigh of relief, feeling that she might just as easily have vaporized and slipped through a slamming door, or jumped from where she was up to the moon. She was speechless.

"Oh, my." Eve put her arms around René, hugging her close. "It's sure better than me having to leave you here with nothing," she said. "Good grief. Just the thought of it." She stepped back and looked at René, holding on to her by the shoulders. "If you don't like it, you can always look around for something else. But I think you're going to love it. I think we can thank our lucky stars."

And just like that, René was set up in New York City. She'd start as a paid apprentice at a mostly non-defunct ballet company now resident in Venezuela. It certainly could have been worse.

"It'll still be expensive," Eve cautioned. "You'll need money for rent and groceries. But at least we won't have to pay for classes, which is saying something. You might even end up with a little extra." She laughed, then grew pensive. "I'm sure it'll be all right." She stopped. "Look at you. We have to celebrate. I'm just so proud!"

Eve ran off to the little kitchen and came back with a box of Entenmann's powdered sugar jelly donuts marked with René's name and room number.

"I can't eat those," René said. "God, Mom." She laughed. "No way."

"Just one," Eve said. "One's not going to hurt you."

"Okay. Maybe one," René echoed. "One last one."

And they laughed and broke open the box.

71

Eve stayed in town for another week. She'd be in the little tenth-floor kitchenette making dinner when René returned from classes each night, pale and spent. There'd be pork chops and salad, or baked chicken and cut-up fruit, or burgers and fried potatoes, all of which, René half joked—still in her ballet clothes, too tired and sore to change—was "no help."

"You have to eat. You need your energy," Eve would say, wrapping up the leftovers. "These'll be here in the freezer for you after I leave, remember."

On Eve's last day she made a tuna casserole, and after dinner they sat together in the common room watching *Happy Days* on the little black-and-white television—René's legs stretched across Eve's lap, Eve massaging the knots in René's calves. And when it was time for bed, they hugged good night, Eve rocking René side to side like she used to do in their kitchen back home.

Eve's flight home was early. She'd be gone before René was even awake.

And they went off to their separate rooms calling back and forth like trilling birds, "Miss you, honey." "Miss you." "Love you, honey." "Love you, Mom."

72

THE NEXT MORNING, AS RENÉ FOLDED HER BED back into a couch—making just enough space for her to stand up in her room—things were already different. The air had a metallic taste she hadn't noticed before, and the hallways were ringing, the overhead fluorescent lights buzzing. She realized with a shock that, from now on, if she were to say something—like *Good morning!* or *How'd you sleep?*—there'd be no one to hear it, no one to answer.

She went into the kitchen and put a slice of bread into the toaster, listening as one of the residents padded off to the communal shower stalls—a single metal door creaking, then slamming shut. She ate her breakfast, grabbed her dance bag, and waited for the elevator to take her down to the lobby, looking off to the room where, just hours before, Eve had been sleeping.

And when the elevator arrived—with a *ding* that shook her from daydreams she didn't realize she was having: the ghost of Eve in the kitchen, getting dinner ready; Eve on the telephone in the hallway, coming up with plans; Eve-the-daring on the dark streets of New York that first night, getting groceries—

a nun in a full-length habit stepped out with her arms full of clean folded sheets.

The nun gave René a quick "G'morning," then walked briskly over to Eve's door and, jangling her keys, turned the knob, stepping into what René could see was now an empty room.

Outside, the streets were knife-edged and electric, full of menace and promise, the slice of sky visible at the end of Seventy-second Street reflecting the color of polished metal. Which meant what? A storm? She had no way of knowing. The light breeze, filled with the new-day smells of the city—traffic exhaust, subway vents, concrete, brick, spoiled liquor, distant smoke—didn't carry even a hint. But not getting any warning didn't mean that whatever was coming wasn't coming.

This jangly, unreadable city, this city of lethal extremes—perfectly coifed women dressed head to toe in French couture stepping into sleek black cars as tattered, piss-soaked street ladies wearing cardboard shoes and cursing into the air pushed shopping carts filled with useless junk all tied up with cord; old buildings of quiet refinement standing glorious in a momentary beam of sunlight as the overflowing dumpsters in the alleyways ran with rats—was hers now. With everyone and everything she'd ever known behind her, this would be her home, and these would be her choices, too—do or die—the streets a perfect mirror.

And though it looked as if she might have a real chance here, a shot at what she'd aspired to for so long from so far away, nothing could be known. Like the storm that was now either imminent or nonexistent, anything was possible because everything was possible.

Still, win or lose, here she was.

Somehow, through everything, she'd earned a place for herself. Not that she could win anything for anyone or make anyone happy, but maybe someday, far off in the future, she'd find a way to make it up to Eve and Al—to let them know she could see all they were doing for her: how hard they were working, how far outside of everything they'd ever known they'd been willing to reach. And she wasn't "taking it lightly," as Eve might say. Maybe someday, she'd find a way to thank them—*yes, Eve, especially*—for letting her go, for giving her this chance.

She had everything she needed. Eve had made sure. And she was here—where she'd so often imagined herself, where she'd fought so hard to be—only just this moment, once again, at her very beginning.

She picked up her pace, feigning self-assurance, weaving swiftly through the other pedestrians, the sidewalk in front of her—pitiless and glistening—opening up, as if to make way.

Acknowledgments

First, I'd like to thank Naomi Goodheart, my editor at Penguin Random House, for her kindness, for her keen eye and astute critical notes, all of which made the manuscript larger and better, and for her help at every step along the way. I feel lucky to have her in my corner. My thanks as well to the whole team at Random House, including Andy Ward, Andrea Walker, Evan Camfield, Annette Szlachta-McGinn, Kelly Winton, Rachel Ake, Jo Anne Metsch, Rachel Parker, Madison Dettlinger, and so many others.

I'd like to extend great thanks to my many readers, especially Mary Karr, for the time she so generously spent going through this manuscript with me when it was much longer than it is now. Thank you, Mary, for your candor, brilliance, and unwavering support. My deepest thanks also to Kathryn Anderson and to my sister, Sara Holcombe, both of whom read many times over, each consistently offering encouragement and insight. Along with these, I'd like to thank Meg Wolitzer, Tom Jenks, Karen Parrish, and Kathy Chetkovitch for their time, inspiration, and generosity in reading. And finally, I have to thank my dear husband, George, for always making himself available to read "just one more time"—again and again. How lucky am I to have him not just as a reader but as a constant companion, the sweetest, kindest heart of my heart. So lucky, and boundlessly grateful.

I'd like to thank my agent, Esther Newberg, who's also been a tremendous reader for me—always zeroing in on the manuscripts I send and never giving up. Thank you, Esther, for your friendship through these many years and for sticking with me through this long process.

My thanks and love, always, to my South Dakota family, those here and gone—Rosemary, Elwood, Mark, and Sara—for their unfailing love and support, and to our next-door neighbor growing up, now the brilliant photographer Stewart Shining, for his friendship and ever-generous spirit.

And most of all, from the bottom of my heart, I want to thank my daughters, Caitlin and Alena, whose deep love and understanding, expansive conversation, and warm embrace are like the sustaining air, opening up vast horizons, making everything possible.

ABOUT THE AUTHOR

PAULA SAUNDERS grew up in Rapid City, South Dakota. She is a graduate of the Syracuse University creative writing program, and was awarded a postgraduate Albert Schweitzer Fellowship at the State University of New York at Albany, under Schweitzer chair Toni Morrison. Her first book, *The Distance Home,* was longlisted for the Center for Fiction First Novel Prize and named one of the best books of the year by *Real Simple.* She lives in California with her husband. They have two grown daughters.

ABOUT THE TYPE

This book was set in Garamond, a typeface originally designed by the Parisian type cutter Claude Garamond (c. 1500–61). This version of Garamond was modeled on a 1592 specimen sheet from the Egenolff-Berner foundry, which was produced from types assumed to have been brought to Frankfurt by the punch cutter Jacques Sabon (c. 1520–80).

Claude Garamond's distinguished romans and italics first appeared in *Opera Ciceronis* in 1543–44. The Garamond types are clear, open, and elegant.